*My Heart on My Sleeve*

Other short fiction anthologies available from
www.honno.co.uk

*All Shall Be Well*
*Coming Up Roses*
*Cut on the Bias*
*Laughing Not Laughing*
*My Cheating Heart*
*Safe World Gone*
*Written in Blood*

# My Heart on My Sleeve

14 stories of love from Wales

Edited by Janet Thomas
Translations by Cathryn Charnell-White

HONNO MODERN FICTION

Published by Honno

'Ailsa Craig', Heol y Cawl, Dinas Powys, South Glamorgan,
Wales, CF64 4AH

1 2 3 4 5 6 7 8 9 10

A catalogue record for this book is available from The British Library.

Published with the financial support of the Welsh Books Council.

ISBN 978-1-906784-66-9

Cover image: Getty Images
Cover design: Graham Preston
Text design: Elaine Sharples
Printed by Gomer Press

# Contents

| | | |
|---|---|---|
| Siân James | *Luminous and Forlorn* | 1 |
| Jane Ann Jones | *Pilgrims* | 13 |
| Siân Melnagell Dafydd | *Rapture on the Rue Nollet* | 31 |
| Angharad Penrhyn Jones | *The Vegetable Beds* | 53 |
| Francesca Rhydderch | *Welsh Gold* | 67 |
| Zillah Bethell | *The Parrot House* | 76 |
| Sarah Todd Taylor | *The Jiltmaker* | 91 |
| Catriona Stewart | *Two Right Hands* | 102 |
| Catherine Merriman | *Painting Juliet* | 110 |
| Jo Mazelis | *The Guilty Party* | 121 |
| Dilys Cadwaladr | *The Foolish Maid* | 131 |
| Jo Verity | *Endings* | 136 |
| Patricia Duncker | *The Madonna at the Midland* | 146 |
| Sarah Jackman | *Leaves and Geese* | 163 |

# *Introduction*

*She had knelt next to the grave of one of these abbots. There, in the afternoon sunshine, the certainty that she need never worry again came to her.*

*Love was eternal and everything was good. 'Oh, God,' she prayed, 'let me always remember this.'*

*But her faith was so weak that she wept that night in his arms.*

*From* 'Pilgrims' *by Jane Ann Jones*

There haven't been many subjects more universal than love, since people began telling stories. Yet 'love stories' has become a tarnished phrase, implying easy solutions and improbably wealthy boys-next-door. Some authors who kindly contributed stories for this collection were initially uncomfortable with having their work described as a 'love story'. But love as a subject inspires writing, as you'll see here, from all sides of life – intense, gentle, funny and cynical. As it always has, the theme of love provokes writers to dig into fallible secret hearts and desires. The title, *My Heart on My Sleeve*, comes from my belief that all these stories are about people at their most vulnerable. There are no easy solutions here…

In some ways, the collection started for a simple, personal reason – I wanted to read 'Pererinion' by Jane Ann Jones, written in 1941, which Honno had published as part of a collection of her stories in its Welsh Classics series, but my

Welsh wasn't good enough to do it justice. I was struck by the Welsh language committee's clear enthusiasm for the story, and by how it came to be written: Jane Ann Jones gave her one paper copy to her ex-lover to read, and when he burnt it she wrote it all again. The writing shines with that determination, that sense that this is a story the writer needed to tell. I am very grateful to Cathryn Charnell-White for her beautiful translations of 'Pererinion' (or 'Pilgrims') and the gentle, bittersweet 'The Foolish Maid' by Dilys Cadwaladr, and delighted to see both stories available in English for the first time.

I am equally grateful to the twelve contemporary authors who have contributed stories to this collection. It was a joy to receive each one. There are ten new stories and two much loved ones, from Siân James and Catherine Merriman, published in previous Honno books. Together they form a rich, diverse collection. As well as their intelligent human insights into relationships, these are also stories that wear their love of Wales and of language on their sleeves.

The stories are grouped from younger to older experience, beginning with the disappointments of a teenage relationship, working through first love, marriage, divorce and affairs, missed opportunities and declarations never made, to end with a range of views of love in later life, love in conflict with the beat of time. I have kept tightly to the theme of romantic love, not including stories that are primarily about the love we have for family and friends. But Patricia Dunker's story, one of her brilliant current series featuring representations of the Virgin

Mary, hints at a wider, stranger world influencing and yet beyond all our human relationships.

Whatever all our happiness and failures mean, I want to end with this simple but beautiful idea from Sarah Jackman,

*'But you know what, love?' Gina's voice is soft, as if it's travelled a long way to reach me. 'It was an odd and beautiful thing, whatever it was. And I'm glad we saw it.'*

*Janet Thomas, January 2013*

# Luminous and Forlorn

## Siân James

'You can come to my place tonight,' Neville whispered to me before school on Monday. 'My parents are having a night out. What do you say? We can have some wine and some beans on toast and we'll dance after. What do you say?'

'Oh Neville, I don't know. I've got my Milton essay to finish and you know I'm only allowed out on Saturday.'

His eyes hold mine. 'Make some excuse. Say there's something on. Something educational. Come on. We'll have a great time.'

He squeezes my hand before I rush off to my prefect duties. Neville is incredibly handsome. He looks like a young Cary Grant. Everyone says so. Eyes brown as toffee and the same cleft in the chin. All the same, I know I won't be able to persuade my mother to let me go out with him on a Monday.

She's never met Neville, but even so, she's dead set against him, her lips becoming thin as little whips whenever I mention his name.

His family is English, which is bad enough, and they keep a licensed restaurant – which is worse. 'Pubs are one thing,' my mother says. 'Pubs are the known enemy. But when cafés,

1

which have always been decent places where decent people can go, start to offer alcoholic drinks, well, it's the thin end of the wedge and a trap to the unwary.'

The way my mother brings out 'alcoholic drinks' you know it's no use trying to break it to her that Neville is your boyfriend.

She doesn't object to you having 'friends of the opposite sex', but she won't have anything serious that might put you off your studies, mind. And in any case, she wouldn't have Neville. What she'd really like is if I still went out to the pictures with Nia Gruffydd every Saturday night, because Nia Gruffydd is one of those girls who wear pleated skirts and hair bands and no trace of make-up. Oh, she's nice enough, but I often wonder if she isn't a bit retarded. She's the same age as me, going on seventeen, but she looks fourteen, with a chest instead of a woman's body, and her idea of a good time is to go to hear Cor-y-Castell rehearsing.

Anyway, my mother idolises her, because her mother writes articles in the *Cymro* and gives talks on the wireless.

'If you pass your exams and go to University, you can become a WEA lecturer like Nia Gruffydd's mother,' she's always saying.

Nia's got a brother called Garmon and I'm sure my mother's secret dream is that he'll fall for me one day. She's always asking after him. He's in his second year at Bangor doing Welsh and Philosophy or something, and of course a safe, long-distance courtship by letter would suit her down to the ground.

'Garmon's going back at the weekend,' Nia tells me in History, which is our first lesson. It's funny, but she's really fond of her brother, though he's so fat and sweaty. Once I called for

2

her and the sitting-room ponged of feet, which must have been him, because whatever you say about Nia, her personal habits are exemplary.

'Would you and Garmon like to come to a party tonight?' I ask her.

'A party?'

Her big round eyes seem about to pop out of her head. For a moment I imagine two lumps of blue jelly landing on her history textbook.

'A party,' I say, trying to sound cool. 'At Neville's. His parents are going out. We can have sandwiches and wine. And we can dance.'

'I can only do the quickstep,' Nia says. 'Don't ask me to rock-around-the-clock, will you.'

We both smile. Sometimes I think the girl's got the beginning of a sense of humour.

Miss Mathias comes in then and just before we settle down to the Repeal of the Corn Act 1842, I feel a cold shiver at my cunning. I've managed it. Got my way again. My mother would never refuse to let me go to a party with Nia and Garmon Gruffydd.

Neville doesn't seem to mind that I've asked Nia and her brother to join us. 'More the merrier,' he says. 'Brynmor's coming along as well. To play the piano.'

I toss my hair back – it's something I've been practising in the mirror. 'Brynmor's always following us around. He's got a piano at home.'

3

'I know. But his mother doesn't like him playing dance music.'

Poor dab. Brynmor's mother is worse than mine. Not only chapel three times every Sunday, but prayer meeting and Band of Hope as well.

All the same, I wish he didn't follow us about everywhere, it's inhibiting for one thing, and humiliating too.

Neville and I park ourselves in one of the little shelters on the prom for a snog, and bloody Brynmor turns up and stands about in front of us and starts talking about Yeats or Schubert or someone, as though that's what we're there for. I suppose it's worse for Nev than me because he doesn't have the slightest interest in poetry or music. God, I never mind having a natter with Brynmor at the right time and place, but when you're sprawled out over somebody, hoping for some sort of vibrant sensual experience, it's just not on.

'Brynmor, go away, will you?'

And what I really can't take is that it's usually me, not Neville, begging him to take the long walk on the short pier.

When you come to think of it, Neville is pretty half-hearted as a lover. His kisses, for instance, are so long and gentle that I could honestly plan out my homework while they're going on and sometimes do. On and on, never changing gear, never reaching any next step.

He never even tries to stroke my breasts, doesn't even try to locate them.

Perhaps I'm lacking in something. Everyone whistles at me, but when I'm in a clinch with someone, they don't half get apathetic.

4

Islwyn Ellis, the boy I went out with before Neville, at least he used to get a bit excited when he started fiddling with the buttons of my blouse. Only when he's managed to get them undone, he always started grunting, and in the dark I used to imagine he'd turned into a little pig and used to push him away. At least Neville is handsome and six foot tall and at least he doesn't grunt.

My mother is one of those people who's always full of jolly little precepts like, 'It's up to the girl to say no.'

My God, chance would be a fine thing.

'How would you feel on your wedding night,' my mother asks me, 'if you'd already given away your greatest treasure?'

My God, no one's ever made any serious bid for my greatest treasure. It'll be really great having to admit that on my wedding night.

Neville rings me every single evening, hangs about me every lunchtime, writes me long, boring letters with terrible spelling when he thinks I'm in a bad mood, but as for his love-making, it's nothing short of pathetic. Do I really want to go on going out with him? Sometimes his five-minute kisses make me feel I could be doing something else. Like running a mile for instance.

Why do people force you into telling lies? I feel really depressed at having to give my mother all that stuff about Nia and Garmon. 'Garmon is very keen that I go with them. He's going back to college next week.' I can imagine her planning her announcement to Mrs Williams next door. 'Yes, she's got engaged, Mrs Williams *fach*. To Garmon Gruffydd. Yes. Delia Gruffydd's son. Her that's on the wireless every Sunday night in '*Wedi'r Oedfa*'. Yes, her only son. Oh yes, Mrs Williams, Welsh to the fingertips. No, Baptist actually, but as long as it's chapel, Morris and I don't mind.'

Why do people make it so difficult for other people, when all they want is to be truthful and decent?

I take ages getting ready. It's not that I want to look particularly terrific or anything like that. It's just that everything is suddenly a bit of a drag. I've made some notes for my *Lycidas* essay and I wouldn't really mind staying in and being able to get to grips with it.

I hope to God I'm not going to turn into one of these intellectual types. Someone in a Welsh tapestry two-piece who's into *cyd-adrodd*. Anyway, I don't look like one. Not yet. As a matter of fact I look more like a photographer's model tonight, my breasts pulled up high in front of me in my new Lovable bra. I could be in the running for Miss Cambrian Coast next year, only of course my mother wouldn't hear of me going in for it. So common.

'Yes Mam, I'll be back by eleven. Don't worry, will you. Yes, I'll be all right.'

Of course I bloody will. Same as ever.

I dawdle along the prom.

It's September and the town is ours again; the two chip shops and the milk bar almost empty.

6

The tide is out and the seaweed smells green and rich. Usually I only like staring out to sea when I've got an ice cream to lick; the cold sweet taste of ice cream goes really well with the tangy smell of the sea. (I love smelling, and eating; all the vulgar pleasures.)

Tonight the sea is calm, its colour almost all drained away. Whitish sky and pale grey sea. But with light in it. Luminous is a brilliant word. I often use it in essays.

I nearly drowned by those rocks when I was about thirteen.

I was allowed to swim from the first of May, and that year, even though the weather turned cold and stormy, I couldn't make myself wait any longer.

No one else was stupid enough to join me.

God, I must have been mad. After only a few seconds I knew I was in danger. The waves were so high that I couldn't go on swimming. The sea kept sucking me up and throwing me down again and after four or five times, I remember the realisation seeping through me that there was absolutely nothing for it but to give up.

But the very next wave threw me against those rocks and I was able to scramble to my feet and stand there, gulping and gasping like a fish in a bucket.

Even wading back was difficult. It was as though the sea was having seconds thoughts about letting me go.

When I got to the beach, there was a man standing there; in a brown tweed overcoat. I remember, 'You bloody fool,' he said. That's all. 'You bloody fool.'

I pulled my towel round me and was sick, almost at his feet. I remember the sand steaming as I covered it up.

I remember my cotton vest scratching like emery paper as I pulled it on.

Even my face was bruised by the pebbles the sea had flung at me.

I told my mother I'd had a fall.

Tonight, there's only the faintest breeze ruffling the luminous water.

'The Bay Restaurant. Licensed to sell alcoholic beverages.' Neville's house is the last on the prom; tall and grey with flashy red paint. A notice in the window. Closed.

Even from across the road I can hear Brynmor Roberts playing away. That old one, 'Begin the Beguine'. For a moment I stand listening. It sounds restless and forlorn with the seagulls mewing in the background. Forlorn is another of my favourite words.

Brynmor is a bit of a joke at school because he composes oratorios which we have to sing in Assembly. But he can certainly play Cole Porter. He can play proper music too for that matter, Beethoven and that lot. He improvises a little fanfare when I go in.

Garmon Gruffydd is sitting at one of the tables with a half-full bottle of red wine in front of him. 'Come to join me,' he says, his voice full and fruity like Mr Issacs, the minister.

They've got a bit of a dance floor in the middle of the room, and what do you know, Neville is there cheek-to-cheek with my little pal Nia Gruffydd. And gosh, Nia is looking almost pretty. She's washed her long straight hair and it's yellow as

Madeira cake and she's wearing it in a loose pageboy instead of tied back like a kid. She's got a pale blue angora wool sweater on and, so help me, she's even got little pointy breasts under there.

I'm usually in a tearing fury if any girl so much as glances as Neville, but tonight I feel tolerant, even good-humoured. The thing is, they look really happy together. He seems much more relaxed with her than he does with me and she's gazing up at him as though she's Cinderella and it's two minutes to twelve. When the music stops, they start walking over towards me but I raise my glass and smile at them and Brynmor launches into something else and they go on dancing and staring at each other.

I take a swig of the wine Garmon's poured out for me. It doesn't seem all it's cracked up to be in poetry; that wine and roses stuff. In fact it tastes a bit like Gee's Linctus. I suppose it's about as romantic as cocoa if you think of it as alcoholic beverage. I drink about half a glassful and then Garmon asks me to dance.

I get to my feet, neither eager nor reluctant. Garmon is certainly not the most desirable partner in the world, but what choice have I got?

He dances quite well, but I wish I didn't keep thinking about his podgy little hands on my back. He does some fancy turns and breathes down my neck. How much of the alcoholic beverage has he drunk, I wonder? And his mother the champion of total abstinence. I feel quite sorry for Mrs Gruffydd, her son on the red stuff and her daughter in the arms of Neville Cooper of no fixed religion, whose one ambition in life is to get his O-level Maths so that he can join the Marines.

It becomes clear that I'm going to have to dance with Garmon all evening. Well, it would be unfair to expect Nia to dance with her brother I suppose. Especially when she's looking so many fathoms deep in love with my bloody Neville. But does ghastly Garmon have to press me so tight? Yes, I know about holding your partner close, but this is suffocation. And when I draw in a deep breath, expanding my chest, the nasty little slug gets the idea I'm being provocative.

'I bet you're hot stuff,' he says, nibbling my ear.

'And I bet you're never going to find out,' I say, breaking away from him and pushing him backwards into a chair.

'I'm going home,' I tell Brynmor.

'I'll get Nev.'

I look over where he and Nia are sitting close together, drinking lemonade.

'No, leave him be. He's happy.'

'I'll come with you then.'

'OK. Neville won't notice.'

We let ourselves out into the silent town. 'I didn't know you were nice as well,' Brynmor says.

Why should I bother to flirt with Brynmor? 'As well as what?' Why should I say it? I know that I'm competently put together and prettily coloured-in too; brown hair, brown freckles, blue eyes, pink nipples.

When we get to the pier, we stand listening to the sea

dribbing onto the pebbles. 'Do you know the Sea Symphony,' he asks me, 'by Vaughan Williams?' His head moves in time to some forlorn music.

'"For Lycides is dead",' I say, '"dead ere his prime."' Tears sting my eyes. I want to live for ever.

'Debussy,' Brynmor says, 'Franz Mahler, César Franck.' He sounds like someone praying.

'"Who would not sing for Lycidas? He knew himself to sing and build the lofty rhyme. He must not float upon his watery bier unwept and … something in the parching winds".'

'Welter,' Brynmor says.

'Yes. "He must not float upon his watery bier unwept and welter in the passing winds".'

'I might set that to music,' Brynmor says. 'Cello and a lot of percussion. Milton's *Lycidas* in E minor.'

'I nearly got drowned once,' I tell him. 'Out by those rocks … of course I shouldn't have gone in. It was very stormy.'

A moment's silence. 'Anyone can make a mistake,' he says then.


We turn towards the town. Terrace Road, Bath Street. Past the chapel where he plays the organ. He tells me I can come to listen to him practising. Anytime.


Our shadows go before us. Brynmor used to be a midget, but now he's nearly as tall as I am. Curly-haired and eagle nosed. 'It was a good party,' he says after a while, 'but I don't think I'm going to come all the way up Penglais with you.'

11

'That's OK,' I say. 'It's no distance from here.'

For a moment we lean against the wall of a house in Maesderw Road and watch the moon come out from behind a cloud and the sky lighten. 'Farewell sweet prince,' I say then, and start to run up the hill. I can still hear sea music in my head, and I'm alive, alive.

# *Pilgrims*

**Jane Ann Jones**
*translated by Cathryn Charnell-White*

1.

'Tell me, where shall we go next?

The Girl was utterly content with the little world they now inhabited. It was a magical country and far from their usual haunts.

Here, the inhabitants were neither Welsh nor English, and their more leisurely way of life had already eased their own troubles somewhat. Although each tried to conceal from the other the heart's fears, those fears were obvious enough to them both. Last night, hadn't the Man pretended that he was nipping out to fetch tobacco and the Girl knew that he was going to the Post Office to send a card to his Wife?

They had been planning this journey for many months, and it was the Girl who determined that they would start in Radnorshire. They had stayed in the region one October six years ago and, although they were only there for three days, the memory of those days intensified continually in the Girl's heart. There, in the troubled months while she waited for the birth of her child, she had experienced the only contentment that she'd known during that difficult period. This time they had failed to find lodgings in the lonely riverside hotel; but they had a meal there, and the Girl had a chance to kneel on a bench and look once again through the window into the room where, that October, she had been knitting and he had been reading in the evening, exactly as though they had year after quiet year to enjoy together.

In that garden, with her hand in his, he had whispered, 'There's no such thing as Time, *'nghariad i*.'[1]

Yesterday, they walked again to the far end of the garden where the river flowed.

It was her who said this time, 'There's no such thing as Time.'

And the pain and doubts of the last six years disappeared with the sound of his words.

As she crossed the lawn, the Girl remembered how the hotelier, while she sat on a bench, brought a piece of wood to put under her feet lest the morning hoar-frost should harm her.

'I wonder where he is now?' she said.

'I'll ask when I go to pay. I might as well go now, for that matter.'

As she waited for him in the car, the Girl imagined that this hotel was created only for them; that it had been waiting for them all these years.

---

[1] *'Nghariad i*: my love.

14

He started the car.

'Well, the poor old fellow has gone the way of all the world.'

'What? He's not dead?'

'Yes, a year ago. He had cancer.'

The Girl tried to have one more look at the house and the garden. So, other dramas had been acted out here, and she was saddened as she thought about the last act in the story of the kindly hotelier.

The Man knocked his pipe.

'You still haven't answered my question,' he said.

She smiled at him apologetically.

'You know, I feel as though I want to remember every minute of these days for ever. Will you promise me that you too will always remember the bells of Kington church ringing tonight, us in Llanfair Waterdine yesterday and …'

'Hey, hold on, you're starting to get sentimental. Come on to bed, *hen chwaer*.[2] I can see I'm not going to get much sense out of you tonight.'

## 2.

'And here, again, is a brand new country,' said the Girl as she looked around.

All of Ceredigion was below them, and the Teifi river ran like a silver thread through the land.

---

[2] *Hen chwaer*: sweetheart.

'What did that boy say this hill was called?' she asked.

'Pen y Bannau, I think. Come on, we'll rest later on.'

They both climbed arm in arm.

'Are you happy, *mêt bach*?'[3]

'Do you have to ask?'

'If I live to be a hundred,' thought the Girl, 'I could never be happier than I am now. Is it, after all, a state of mind? And why can't I always be like this?'

She looked at his face and gave a small sigh. Yes, her happiness relied entirely on being in his company. Oh God, she asked for so little … only to be with this man.

He heard the sigh.

'What's the matter with you, *was*?[4] Tired?'

She smiled at him. Now was not the time to raise the same old problems.

'Come on, make yourself comfortable. We can rest for at least an hour.' And he pulled out his pipe.

The Girl looked towards the valley below.

'Who'd have thought Strata Florida was so beautiful!'

They had come across Strata Florida completely unexpectedly.

Seeing the name Pontrhydfendigaid on a signpost had caused him to slow the car down.

'Pontrhydfendigaid,' he read slowly.

---

[3] *Mêt bach*: little friend.

[4] *Was*: my dear.

'Blimey!' he said afterwards, 'Strata Florida must be nearby. Would you like to see the place?'

Until now, Strata Florida was to her a charming name on a map.

This minute she remembered how she had come across the name on a map in one of the school's Welsh books.

As they both walked along the lane, he tried to remember Hedd Wyn's lines to the place.

'Bother! They're on the tip of my tongue too – something about "cnwd o fwsog melfed" [a covering of velvet moss].'

But she could not help. Neither he nor she knew then Gwynn Jones's lovely words:

*Pan rodiwyf ddaear Ystrad Fflur,*
*O'm dolur ymdawelaf.*
[When I walk the ground of Strata Florida,
I will find peace from my pain.]

But a time would come when the memory of them standing for a while at this place would be balm to her soul.

*A deuddeng Abad yn y gro*
*Yn huno yno'n dawel.*
[And twelve Abbots there in the earth
sleeping quietly.]

She had knelt next to the grave of one of these abbots. There, in the afternoon sunshine, the certainty came to her that she need never worry again.

Love was eternal and everything was for good. 'Oh God,' she prayed, 'let me always remember this.'

But her faith was so weak that she wept that night in his arms.

'Oh! What'll I do? What'll I do? I can't live without you.'

He tried to calm her.

'*'Nghalon i*,[5] try to be thankful for what we have.'

But there was no comfort for her in his words. Only sleep eased the pain.

## 3.

'We'll have to come this way again,' said the Girl.

They had both doted at the Pembrokeshire coast.

'Newport,' she wrote shakily in her diary as they went past that lovely little place.

'This is where we'll come,' she said. 'If we could only see each other for one week a year, life would be worth living.'

He too was trying to take solace from the idea that they would have a time like this again. As he drove the car, he looked at the girl writing at his side. Had he, he wondered, ruined her life? But it was too late now to think of such a thing. And what about his Wife, who was spending her holiday with friends fifty miles away from him? Fifty miles. Fifty miles. But that distance was always between them, in spite of her attempts to get closer to him. 'Oh God, how many more lives will I ruin?'

---

[5] *'Nghalon i*: my heart.

'What's the matter with you? You look serious. Do you need a drink?'

'It's you, more likely, that wants tea. We'll look for somewhere now.'

Over their tea, he said, 'Since we're in this part of the country, what would you think if we called at St. David's? I've never been there before, and they do say that every Welshman should visit at least once in his lifetime.'

She was utterly content. Being with him anywhere was her heaven.

Like the thousands of pilgrims before them, they felt a warm thrill as they, all of a sudden, came across this beautiful old building. They did not want anyone to guide them and maybe, as a result, they missed much valuable information, but they gained something else that they would never lose.

'Look up,' he whispered.

They both wondered at the exquisiteness of the ceiling and marvelled too at the beauty of the coloured glass.

In St. David's chapel a young priest was kneeling.

They both stood watching him.

'Is he ...' began the Girl.

'Sh!' said the Man, pulling her away.

In the car, she insisted that such worship was something purely external.

He was not so sure.

'He was only young,' she continued. 'Do you think it's right that he should renounce all of life's pleasures? We're here to live.'

'We know nothing of his history, but I would swear that that

19

man was honest. Did you see how pale he was? You can't look like that without having wrestled with something significant.'

'But don't you think that it's a sin to turn one's back on life?'

'But, *'nghariad i*, what is life? I don't know. I only know that, when I'm with you, I feel alive, but maybe it's some defect in me that means that life isn't always a real thing for me. There's such a thing as the life of the spirit, you know.'

She winced, as always, when she heard him talking about the life of the spirit.

As the car sped along the main road, she became tired and had great difficulty in staying awake, but after reaching the hotel and smelling the good food they were both revived.

Over their wine, she said, 'Aren't you glad that you can enjoy these?'

He raised his glass and his smile was answer enough.

'I think it's a sin not to enjoy everything in life.' As he spoke the priest's face appeared before his eyes.

'What enjoyment does that priest get from renouncing all and worshipping?'

'It seems that's the only way he feels pleasure.'

'Good gracious!' she said, and changed the conversation.

In bed that night, as she lay herself down to sleep at his side, in that moment between sleep and wakefulness she saw again that pale face.

A shiver coursed through her body and she moved closer to him. He had felt her move and they both turned towards one another. He too was trying to escape from the pale face.

# 4.

'Aren't you ready yet?'

'You two make a start. I'll come after you directly,' the Wife called to her friends who were waiting for her at the bottom of the stairs.

'Okay then. You know where to find us – on the pier.'

She heard the front door of the lodging house close after them. Although they didn't know it, she was perfectly ready to start out, and she sat at the window in the bedroom to watch for the postman. As a rule, the afternoon post arrived about four, and today they had decided to have tea in a new café on the pier. She must set off, she must indeed. She would be back within an hour or two and she could wait until then, surely, for a letter or a card from the man she had married eighteen years ago. Once again, she held back. She got up to look at herself in the mirror. There, she saw a woman who was neither young nor old.

'I suppose I'm middle aged,' she said to herself.

'And this is what being middle aged is,' she then said, looking intently at her own image. There was not as much colour in her hair and cheeks now, and there were little tiny furrows near her eyes.

'But from afar …' she said, and moved back a step. No, there wasn't much wrong with her as she looked at herself from here. She had not had children and she had managed to keep her shape.

Strangely enough, she had never wanted children, and neither had he, according to what he said. But if they'd had children they would not now be spending their holidays apart. For a moment, she saw the Man lazing in a deckchair, a newspaper concealing his face, and she lifting the foot of a little suntanned boy to dry him with a towel … Oh God, where had she gone wrong? Her entire aim in life was to ensure his comfort, but he was getting further away from her all the time.

One part of her tried to imagine him these days wandering cheerily in the company of other men, but some disagreeable voice in the bottom of her heart questioned, questioned perpetually.

'Oh, what will I do, what will I do if he's with some other girl? I won't give him up for anyone. He's mine.' And tears came to her eyes.

'I really mustn't cry at this time of day,' and she tried to smile at the image in the mirror. 'That's better,' she said, and anyone hearing her light, quick steps coming down the stairs when she heard the sound of the postman would not think other than that she was a thoroughly happy married woman.

The kitchen door was half opened.

'Everything's alright, Mrs Jarvis. There was one there for me. I'm running a bit late.'

'Damn the afternoon post,' she said under her breath. But this was to be expected since he was fifty miles away from her; fifty miles …

She tore the sides of the lettercard. ('Why, I wonder, is he so keen on these stupid old lettercards? I'd much prefer a card with a picture of where he is on it than some excuse of a letter like this'.)

After all, there was hardly any point waiting for it. A word or two about the weather; his friends and he had come across a pretty place in Radnorshire, rather too quiet for her perhaps.

('How does he know? He doesn't want to try to get to know me.')

He hoped that she was enjoying herself; he, as usual, sent his best wishes.

Best wishes. Best wishes. Best wishes. She walked to the seaside to the sound of those two syllables, and somehow the sound comforted her. Wasn't the unromantic lettercard proof that he at least remembered her?

## 5.

'I can't go on like this. We must give one another up,' said the Man.

Although the Girl had heard him utter the same words time and time again, the verdict went through her heart like an arrow. It was easy to see that he was serious. There were signs of worry on his face and weariness in his voice.

'Don't worry so much,' he encourged her. 'Leave things be. You see, man is apt to let things take their course over years, but a time comes when he has to choose.'

'And you're choosing to leave me?'

They both looked at each other in the moonlight. The sound of autumn was on the wind, and the Girl drew nearer to him.

'No, don't make things harder, *mêt bach*. Remember, if it's wretched for you, it'll be just as bad, if not worse, for me. It'll be a life of perpetual acting. Will you try to help me?'

She did not reply. 'Why must I act now?' she thought. 'I don't want to give him up and why must I pretend that I'm ready to give this up for something, for someone, God knows what?'

She started to weep when she realised that she couldn't keep him. Why, oh why, did the girl always have to yield to the man's verdict?

'Don't cry, *'nghalon i*. I'll be thinking about you all the time. Remember that, and try to be brave.'

She thought for a moment that her tears would keep him at her side for a while, but he whispered, 'Goodnight, and bless you.' And away he went.

The Girl stayed still for some time. Six years earlier, when she'd had to leave her baby with strangers, and then lost him through death, she had thought then that she could not suffer more, but this minute her heart was as bruised as ever. Wasn't there some medication for such blows? She was ready to admit that she had often felt extreme joy, but now she had nothing or no one to live for. How pleasant it would be to go to sleep tonight without having to wake again! But it seemed that she would spend year after year in solitude, without hope or a song in her heart. If life was a gift to mankind, then she was perfectly ready to do without it. What value was there in living when the best was in the past?

## 6.

The Girl tried to overcome the ache in her heart with every means available to her: through work; by trying to ignore the images and voices of the past; another time through embracing the joy and misery of days gone by in their entirety. But it was all to no avail. To the world, she showed quite a cheerful face and she had a ready answer for everyone who asked, but beneath the surface there was only deep longing and a pervasive barren feeling. She tried to remember all that she'd had, when there was nothing missing, but oh! But oh! It was not enough now to remember the joy that had been. Why could she not feel alive again; once again enjoy the certainty that she experienced in Strata Florida, that life was on her side and everything was for the best?

More than once she was amazed that the pain in her heart could last so long.

The philosophers' words that time healed all pain were too easy.

'Well, if nothing else happens, I'm getting older every day,' she said to herself. 'And that's what I want – to get rid of the years as well as I can.' She knew that there was something unworthy in her attitude towards life, but for the life of her, she could not feel the same zest for reading, chatting, for dealing with the trifles of her everyday life.

One summer she felt an urge to go to the border country on her own.

She was not brave enough to walk again along the old paths, but now and then while wandering through Shropshire, she found herself very near to the places where they had previously been so happy, and she was surprised that seeing a familiar name on a signpost did not cause her more pain than it did. 'Maybe I'm at fault for escaping; maybe I should let the past become a part of the present.' She saw that the past, for good or bad, had made her what she was.

While standing at Ludlow bridge, and gazing at the river below, she remembered how they had both said, in turn, 'There is no such thing as Time.'

And, indeed, when she could afford to stay still, she knew that the things that happened ten years ago were as vivid in her heart as yesterday's sorrow.

The past was pulling her, constantly pulling her, and she felt as though she was being forced to look back, although every day of this lonely journey was full of interest. She liked watching everyone who passed by and, as she took notice of the occasional face, she could almost hear the Man's voice whispering, 'Everyone has a cross to bear in this life, you see.'

And where was he now, she wondered? Oh dear, she must try not to start thinking about him again, but what would she give to hear him, damning his false teeth even? She smiled when she realised that it was even possible to feel longing for a loved one's false teeth.

It was good to have a break like this to put her life in order. By now she could see her foolishness in relying on another for her happiness, as she had done with the Man. It was easy enough in the past to claim that it was not possible to love without having to rely, but she knew now that no one could love or live properly without first being friends with himself. Everyone is lonely, and no matter how far or how often one tried to escape from oneself, one had to return to that self in order to have peace of mind.

Peace of mind! That was now her goal, and after realizing that need, she had been too diligent in her search. It will come like a light shower of rain creating beauty in barren land.

## 7.

The Man and the Wife also went on holiday together that summer, but both were relieved to return home. Not that they hadn't enjoyed themselves, but perhaps they both had tried too hard to be polite.

'Where shall we go today?' he'd ask.

'Oh, anywhere you'd like to go,' she would reply, and neither one was sure whether they had pleased the other.

'Well,' said the Man to himself, on his way out (after a bite to eat) to see what state the back garden was in, 'I knew very well that I'd have a life of acting.' There was plenty to do in the garden but he didn't lose heart. It was much easier acting the contented husband around the house and garden than sitting by his wife on an iron seat for hours on end. His remedy was not to think about the past at all, but although he succeeded, he could never be sure when some image would appear before his eyes to prove that every trick, every detail of the Girl was still in his heart.

He no longer asked the big questions: What is life? What is death? What purpose is there in suffering? He had chosen his lot and it was now enough to live from day to day. He had paid a high price for past pleasures and he must now pay the price for peace of mind. Peace of mind? Was that the prize every man sought? He extinguished his pipe and made a start with the weeding.

Seeing him put his pipe in his pocket, the Wife smiled as she watched him through the bedroom window. She knew that he would now be outside until supper time and she continued unpacking. These past years she knew where he was almost every hour of the day and night, but nonetheless she didn't feel one bit closer to him. He was so careful around her and she had no cause to complain of his behaviour towards her. Indeed, it would be easier to bear if only he grumbled a bit; about the monotony of life; about her, she wished. Despite living so closely to him she barely knew him and now she must learn to live without expecting anything of him. She folded his waistcoat before putting it in the drawer, and smelling his tobacco, a wave of despondency came over her. She, perhaps, was the loneliest of the pilgrims.

8.

'Where are you going this year?' friends asked the Girl.

'I don't know yet. Why?'

'She's a good one,' said one of them, 'for asking "Why?" and it's July already.'

28

Another one said, 'She could enjoy herself in Blaenau Ffestiniog if necessary!'

'And why not?' said the Girl, smiling.

In the evening, as she remembered their challenge, the Girl realized how true their words were. 'I'm a contented creature at last,' she said. She could not tell when she had given up grappling with her lot in life. Indeed, on occasion she had been so busy that she did not have time to consider her condition.

'I've been so foolish,' she said, 'complaining that life was so tedious. The problem was inside me all along.'

She recalled how she sought to be rid of the years, and now they passed too quickly. On the outside, nothing of importance was happening to her. Almost all her friends were married and some had children, but no matter how great their wealth, she felt that her life was just as rich because she could now love without asking for anything in return. Every mother seemed to seek something better for her own child than the children next door, and the tiresome competition left its mark on their lives. Why did they not learn to be content with what they have? wondered the Girl, forgetting how long it took her to learn that every loss that is faced bravely enriches life. Losing in order to win. Yes, she had gained something and that something had come to her completely imperceptibly. Is that how joy comes to the heart? Life was not something to be solemn about but something to take pride in. Every hour is a gift, and all but the foolish embrace it.

It wasn't important where she would go on holiday this year. But one day, one day she would go again to St. David's.

Although she might not, perhaps, arrive in body, she knew that a day would come in her life, as in the life of every pilgrim, when she would experience the peace of that place and know the purpose of all journeying.

*June 1944*

# Rapture on the Rue Nollet

## Siân Melangell Dafydd

Head away from the Sex Supermarkets and Erotic Museums. Go higgledy-piggledy towards Rue des Dames until you find a shop selling sequined women's clothing and sky high kinky boots big enough for men to wear. Hang a right.

Édouard Manet used to take this walk regularly: the artist famous for painting a picnic scene with fashionably dressed men and naked women. As if that wasn't odd enough, he painted them slap bang in the middle of Paris: you can almost identify the individual quirks and knots of the Tuileries trees. Isn't that the classic insecurity dream – being in public, naked? But this painting isn't a dream scene – far from it. There they are, *á poil* with their bread rolls and cherries as if it's the most natural thing in the world. Real people, not pictures of people, not even a little bit pretend, but fleshy. Rays of sun shine through the tree canopy and bounce back from the women's real bare skin. One of them lounges on the grass and the other wades about in the pond like a Grecian goddess come to life. If the men were naked too, that would be something. A bit of equality: all-round madness, skinny dipping in broad daylight. But, no. They're kitted out as fashionably as city gentlemen

31

could be, oblivious to the social humiliation of their women. But maybe it's a case of the King's New Clothes. Queens. Don't tell the women that they're naked or they'll know that they have bodies.

Anyway, the mind behind this immoral painting, Manet, used to come right here in 1852. He was leading a double life, at the time. Before and after setting foot in this street, he was a single man, the son of a Judge, an artist (though some might have quibbled with that part). But as soon as he stepped between these seven storey buildings, onto this patch of Paris, he was a family man, spending time with his Suzanne and his secret son. Take his steps. Enter rue Nollet.

It's evening: almost time for the rose-sellers to come out to make big eyes at anyone looking like they might fall in love, and loiter until someone feels uncomfortable enough to give them two Euros in exchange for privacy and a half-dead rose. At the mouth of the street, the inside of a small café warms up. Many arrive alone, as if the place is only stumble distance from their bedrooms, their minds on the kind of private thoughts you have between wardrobe and shower, fridge and kettle: why do I have so many split ends, I should file my nails, I should dust the TV. One woman is in slippers. Two main things are done here: smoking and drinking. Both are done heavily. Both position lips to look ready to kiss, any second now.

A man tucked in between the bar and the window beams at you and says, 'I wouldn't if I were you.'

Too late, you're in anyway. Let the door close behind you. So, in front of you, here are some chairs from closed down schools. Tables, folded up squares of newspaper under the odd leg here and there to stop the wobbles. Sugar sachets and cigarette butts everywhere but especially in a rim around the serpentine zinc bar through the room. Hooks under the bar for handbags and to bruise knees. Seats by the walls and by the bar are filled up first so the room is lined with limbs: legs (crossed), arms (elbows on tables), the middle tables almost all empty. People need to cling to surfaces, and from there, they look out.

By the back wall, a man bends over his table, nose to the wood as if he's trying to escape the smoke curling thickly about nose and eye level. He presses on his ballpoint as if a direct line went from the notebook to his heart. Breaking the energy circuit would be fatal. He draws cartoons of things that are not here, a squashed-faced dark little boy with spiky hair and a giant black eye, a robot dressed in red ink with the caption, 'Only the toughest robots wear wool.' As he finishes one, he discards it to the unoccupied half of his table, with the half-full sugar sachets and their ripped heads. It's one of those things he does when there's nothing else to do. Others might bite their cuticles or send text messages but his thing is this, drawing companions.

About his head, strong coffee is served on a *planche* (slices of tree trunks, the rings exposed and not polished). It comes in glasses, not cups. That way it cools quicker; dawdlers risk cold coffee (this doesn't really work because here, even if drinks can be downed in one, thoughts come slower and can be pondered above long-empty coffee). Coffees come with two other glasses, one holding brown and white sugar tubes, a spoon thin enough to snap with your own front teeth and a cinnamon stick. The other glass is bigger and is full of lukewarm water. And on some tables, there are ravages of food: cheese and raw meats on a larger *planche*, baskets of bread. Everything for one.

Someone enters. They blink wildly to clear their immediate air. Once their eyes adjust, they do the rounds, kissing the cheeks of whoever is relevant to them. No, that's not quite right. Maybe when they first knew each other, they touched. Now, their kisses have cleaved apart. If you took a photo of the most intimate moment, you'd see two bodies that lean backward away from each other with everything except a reluctant cheek: good enough. Then there are newspapers, suduku, conversations about Sarky or complaints about the price of something or other. Take your pick. Welcome. Sit at the bar.

'Never,' the barman says to the man next to you, 'never fall in love with two people.' This is Luc (do not say Luck). He is advising Jean and something in his voice makes the idea irresistible when he says, 'Just don't do it,' shaking his head.

'Is it possible to?' Jean asks the barman's back as he gets on with cleaning the cappuccino frother. But he needn't ask. It is, now, possible, just because the idea has been aired. A tantalising, entangled problem. Oh, it's real. And it has an exotic impossibility to it. *Two*. Trouble but.

Jean and Luc's lips part as though they've just discovered the bulk and oyster thickness of their own tongues inside their mouths, moving and demanding. They stare back, hard, draining each other's desires and saying nothing, not admitting to their – what is it – greed? An intoxicating, delirious and destructive craving. Jean actually rests his tongue on the corner of his bottom lip where his cigarette would go later.

'I don't think it is,' he says, with his hands on his hips. This is as good as daring Luc to provide examples, of course. Proof of the impossible, go on.

But I won't tell you how the rest of the conversation goes. He has examples all right, but there are also other people in the bar you need to be acquainted with, to get a full picture, for your own safety. Let's crack open a few heads.

Here we go: him where the bar starts, by the door, he's Guillaume. Nobody's sure what he does for a living because he seems to be here all the time but he has plenty of money for drinks. If he got up from his perch, you'd see a Versace eagle on the back pocket of his jeans, though you'd never guess from the state of their front. He's rarely seen out of his seat anyway. He has become Door Keeper over the years. Don't sit on that stool, if it's ever empty. It's his. You should acknowledge and register his advice even if you don't completely follow it.

He says, 'I wouldn't if I were you,' to anyone who orders a *planche* of meat and cheese, putting the palm of his hand on his heart. 'It'll unsettle you.' He eats plenty of them himself – folded up protein, Cantal, Morbier, Comté, into parcels like the newspaper pads propping up table legs; pops them in his mouth, whole, *charcutrie* fat still in strings between his teeth. In his case, it doesn't make any difference. It's far too late for this place or its food to unsettle Guillaume. Immunity: his flesh is made up of this place. But don't dismiss his words, you're not immune, are you? Trust that smile, even if it's threaded with pig fat.

Last week he maybe raped the girl who's sitting by the window: Camille. She's sometimes used that word but only to herself to try it out: it scrapes her insides and she thinks of something else. When she pushes the word from her gut to her throat, it chokes her there. The problem is that she invited him back to hers but she didn't want that. It's just – if it wasn't rape, why did he bolt? He wouldn't have, would he, leaving her nose down on the sofa, if it had all been normal and nice.

She reads.

She has confided, only, in Stephen (I'll get to him later) who said, 'I'm not the one you should be telling.'

But she refused to go through telling it again.

He said she should have done something about it already. She heard: it's too late to do something about it now. Stephen resorted to buying her plenty of Merlot and not buying himself any food the next day or two to balance out his budget. They both woke up with sore heads and walked in for a coffee, together. Now rumour has it that they are secretly together and he doesn't mind.

She puts the book down to fidget with the trinkets that come with coffee, looks out of the window as though she might be waiting for someone, puffs; reads again.

Jean is bonkers about her but she thinks he's bonkers about everyone. Even when he brings over her *planche* of coffee things with the excuse of saving Luc, she blanks him.

36

Next to her (the tables are close here, like most Parisian cafes – personal space is a hair's breadth), so very close by, is Renso, writing. He has achieved two lines so far. He sits there with hair as shiny as his black ballpoint. Apparently he's from Calabria. Sometimes he says he left because he didn't like the sea, other times it was to avoid the Mafia who were after him for something terrible and unspecified. He was on the way to London but by Paris he had a sore bum. He stepped off the train without a single Franc on him and walked in a straight line. He found an Italian restaurant and has never been to London. He is happy, he says, and does not wonder what could have been. He always sticks to the same tale so people assume that's really how he ended up here. Everyone comes from somewhere. If asked what he does, he'll answer, 'I'm a philosopher.' That shuts most people up. The way he runs his fingers through his hair is convincing.

Next: Stephen. He's an unemployed academic, waiting for a job to come along that's worthy of the years he's put in. Meanwhile, he's not putting in any more. People know to offer him a drink but never a slate. He knows, from Camille, that Guilliame doesn't wear underwear. He'd rather not know. Worse still, he also knows that Guilliame waxes his entire body. He'd never have guessed. Guilliame doesn't smell hairless to him.

Then Guilliame kisses Sabine who has just stepped in. She places her Chihuahua on a bar stool, her handbag on a hook and a just-cooled chocolate cake on the zinc. She has her own knife and kitchen roll for sharing. The recipe is her mother's from San Francisco. She was sent back to her family in Paris after getting too involved with cocaine over there. They thought Paris would be cleaner. Although she kept this history to herself for months, it came out the night she collapsed in the toilet and the door had to be ripped off to get help to her. It's thought that she's the one who wrote on the toilet wall: *beware of (name scrubbed out) girls – he's a liar and he can't keep it up, anyway.* She offers the first piece of cake to Guillame.

Francis arrives. He's a successful writer, works for TV, gets up at five in the morning and puts in a day's work before this lot have their first coffee. He never stays in the café long. Kiss, kiss, coffee, go. He has looks on his side. Always, people want him to stay longer. Without a fuss, he wangles two slices of cake.

And among them a choux-pastry-faced woman cowers over a middle table with six empty coffee cups. She wears school shoes, one red sock, one white, and many other things layered under a coat that never comes off. She also wears long, fake pearls over a heavy braless breast. On her table she has a plastic bag of baguette halves: yesterday's. And these were never left in linen towels overnight to keep them from turning into bones. They've long lost their apricot aroma. There's a saying here that if someone's hair is done particularly badly, that it's been styled with a baguette butt-end. Well yes, maybe, in the case of this woman.

Hairstyles age people. A little neglect and they look younger than their age and carefree: children don't do products, diffusers and expensive cuts. Serious neglect and they look older. Hair is all about deception. This woman belongs to the second group: she's beyond caring. In fact, she scarcely seems to inhabit time, as though she was a mistake, just waiting for her story to be concluded justly, for the right combination of coffee cups, people and stories to combine, and then she would vanish.

All six of her coffee glasses have their place and she looks forward and out. Her words are only sounds: half-digested consonants and foreign vowels, as if sadness can turn teeth into dough. She says something long and painful which Luc interprets as a single coffee, so he places one in front of her, with the other empty ones. The story goes, she was fine until a few years ago (articulate, clean, busy, wore a bra). And then, something happened.

Someone lifts a chair over her head and she doesn't notice. Jean is in the middle of reacting to Luc's story, which you've missed by now. Jean repeats, 'Never, never, you're kidding me,' but Luc stands with his hands on his hips, teacloth over his shoulder and says nothing because this is his world and every world has its inner logic. This is his. He surveys his group. They do not know what he knows about them. It's 5pm on a winter's evening and none of his customers seem to have been at work today.

*

It was into this scene, one day, a young British woman walked, un-warned. This is her story:

She needed Wifi. It was as simple as that. So, all she needed was this local café.

'I wouldn't if I were you,' a man said as she entered but she was already in, eyes filling with tears as she adjusted to the level of toxins in the air. This was the first of three warnings the Door Keeper gave her. She didn't want to appear rude.

'Pardon?' she said, shared her name with him and found out what he was called, too, in the process. She didn't remember his name for very long because all the other names in the bar jostled for attention until she forgot most of them and remembered faces. But he she recognised from the onset as the Door Keeper.

This woman had just inherited an interesting sum of money and broke up with her family soon after. She remembered certain things about her grandparents, some things she'd been told, some things she'd assumed and other things she was convinced she really remembered for herself. They married young (story) not really aware of how beautiful they were. He would do things like buy funny postcards for her when she had PMT (evidence existed of this) and she'd squeeze his hand in boring public events (memory). They had a secret code:

'Meet me on the purple hill under the red tree.'

She never knew what this exactly meant. And now, today, she thought of the hill behind her, of Montmartre, up there, gleaming white and gold on the hill, and closed her eyes. But she thought her grandparents' quirks, like this, were signs of genuine sweetness and effortless creativity. She loved her grandfather for them, especially. He died two days after her grandmother – heartache was the official verdict – people said, 'Ah, yes,' and nodded intelligently when they heard they died almost together. And they had been so beautiful; both of them. That word didn't fit many men. 'Handsome' yes. 'Good looking' too. But a 'beautiful' man was a rare thing and carried an aura of strength and lightness like stained glass windows.

As it turns out, both grandparents had lovers who wept at the funeral and couldn't eat the sandwiches or the cakes. Her parents didn't flinch. But she was lucky, she told herself. She was in Paris to find a little city apartment with the money left to her. The hill, maybe. Some place like Amélie's place in that film, with loose floor tiles and old stories in the walls, sandwiched in between streets named after famous sculptors: Breton, Veron, Pilon. She was dizzy. She saw the Moulin Rouge that day and giggled for ten paces because in fact, it was seedy, really ugly, after all that fuss, and she was in on the secret.

She didn't tell the Door Keeper any of this, only the main purpose of her visit. Basic patter. She was buying a pied à terre. Her French was passable so long as she stripped what she really wanted to say down to its bare practicalities.

He said, 'You are charming, charming.' She guessed *charmant*: charming and imagined a procession of charming ants to register the word. And he followed that with, 'But you're going to get into trouble. Try not to, but you will, you will.'

She didn't believe him. This was Europe in the twenty-first century. This was not Beirut. This was not the Moon. She knew the rules. She knew how to take care of herself. *Voila*. Coffee.

She sat down, opened her laptop, took a sip of coffee and connected. Her email home read, simply: *Salut, I am here.*

And she was. She had arrived in a place that became impossible to leave. She popped in for the first coffee of the day, to struggle over a local newspaper and to check the available properties of the day. Then people would happen. Conversations were vital for her to improve and advance with a language that made her feel as intellectually advanced as a six year old. Yes, she was there to find an apartment but as soon as she found herself in the clutches of this café and struggling, another need overtook that one: that of being able to be herself, in French. Not a fumbling stranger. Not shy. Not someone who said what was essential and then shut up. She wanted to be able to waffle and get angry. Her difficulties were charming, charming.

*How's the hunt?* popped up on chat, followed by three 'x's and a digital red rose.

*It's going,* she answered.

*How romantic – my dream. I hope you're having as wonderful a time as I imagine you are. If you have a wild fling with a sexy Frenchman while you're there, I won't say a word, honest. Just don't kiss anyone with a moustache!* ;-)

Her friend's words: sans serif, black on white. The air of home clung to them, Zoë's flat, the desk in the dining room corner, Typhoo in a Purple Ronnie mug, pink light, art deco Laura Ashley curtains and thick carpets. All of those things crammed into the message. And so Zoë wasn't far. And she knew that if she could see Zoë sitting there, giggle-typing, slurping, dreaming; Zoë didn't have a single visual clue to assemble a picture of where she was. For Zoë, she was in a film France. She looked about her: chipped wall plaster, wacky old tiles, blackboards of wine lists in illegible loopy French, light from an old basket covering a bulb. She moved her wine glass so that if it tipped, it was far enough from the keyboard. Zoë wouldn't see this in her emails; they would arrive square. A sculpture of a head made out of, what – a coconut or ball of wood – on top of the microwave. And the smell of dusty cinnamon and smoke-filled woolly jumpers. The black crack in the bar mirror shaped like fangs. Maybe Zoë could imagine a bar, and menus on blackboards, but not all of this.

While she pondered, alone, in a mixture of French and English, she listened to a man's telephone conversation with his friend, Olivier. They were discussing where each was supposed to be. Arguing actually: said *truc* a lot – thing – the thing is; it reminded her of her nephew who called everything 'tractor'. No agreement on what they had or hadn't said before, lots of yes, no, yes, but I didn't say that. Eventually, it was, 'I embrace you,' he said, 'until later, kisses,' and hung up. She felt embarrassed for them and then embarrassed for being embarrassed. Yes, she had understood the words. I embrace you, kisses. This world she had entered was pleasing.

So here, she savoured life and slowed down, marvelled at the bits of stories they fed her, the curious lost souls they were. The bartender who had been on track to be a lawyer and saw the error of his ways, had fallen out of university and into the bed of a woman who sold Clinique moisturiser. She turned out not to be worth it, but the deed was done. And he'd pour her extra wine and bump shoulders with her and laugh. The Italian who said he wasn't Mafia even before he said hello, which must mean that he was. His *pollenta* was like nectar: he fed people with a coffee spoon from a bowl that needed asbestos-fingers to hold, held under a back table one night. Nobody refused.

Tackling a new language made the days timeless. She hesitated over her vocabulary and stuttered over the right pronouns until a sentence that should have taken thirty seconds had in fact taken half an hour. Then, a debate on the true pronunciation of 'une'. It was easier to talk to men. Women sat like cats, had their own communities.

The bartender taught her 'u' – it comes from the throat, not the lips, as in, 'Luc'. There was a delicacy to getting it right, holding sound in a new part of her mouth.

'It's like, you need to carry a grape in the back of your mouth and keep it safe, all night while you talk, drink, everything. Don't squash that grape,' he said, and served wine.

She perfected sentences full of grapes. Accepted drinks. It made the muscles of her mouth softer, gentler on the invisible fruit, softer on her French. But still, this language left a sensation in her mouth like rinsing with vinegar and she stopped trusting her own sounds. A distorted French that was a little bit Spanish, a little bit English and a little bit imitation. She tried. She bloody tried, and got tired. Doubted herself. Lost herself. Part of that could have been the wine. She became fidgety with a glass in her hand. But then someone would fill it up (that Luc was kind, but it was exactly what she didn't need, but she drank, but she was grateful and fidgety). That was a problem here. Some rules were different. Drinks were poured and poured without being paid for, until the end of the night when it was time to own up to how much she'd had and she was too intoxicated to remember. Especially since, at the end of the night, she also had to contend with fending off men who had kindly bought her a drink and now wouldn't go away.

Her sustenance became coffee, wine, smoke. No solids. She felt elegant and light. Started altering her eye make-up, darker. Her reflection developed a frown from listening so hard in a noisy bar. When she collapsed into bed, never before two, exhausted, she didn't recognise her own body. She smelled as though she had a stranger with her. Even when she nuzzled into the cotton sheets, searching for traces of familiarity: no. She considered how, even if she didn't have an apartment yet, she now knew which part of the mouth 'ous' came from compared to 'os'. And what kept her awake was – oh what was it again, that word, the one she learned on the last swig of wine? Her face muscles felt strong in new places. And always, always, she was tired.

She met Gabriel. She remembered him in particular and couldn't think why. There are some men. He spoke English. Maybe that was it. It made his whole body more clearly defined against the rest of them. He had various accents: words over three syllables tended to be more English than Hollywood. He said things like 'indeed' in the right places. They jumped right over the building blocks of first conversations and found themselves deep in conversation about improbable things:

45

goosebumps, lucky charms, vampires. He was beautiful, maybe. She looked at him again: chipped front tooth; the odd wispy white in his beard; but mainly dark, dark all over; his hair overgrown to his shoulders.

She looked at him again and he was looking right back. She blushed. They spoke about the possibility of the French being immune to the power of the word 'love' since they used it for everything: *j'aime ta joupe.* You could 'love' absolutely anything. 'Love' had become 'like'. 'Love' wasn't loaded, wasn't difficult. A quirk in the dictionary affected people's ability to feel. She was sure of it. But she didn't have all the French words in all the right order to explain that idea with anyone else. Their knees touched when they spoke; she sat up straight and made a barrier. Trouble, she told herself, lies this way.

She had a wisp of a conversation with Camille.

'Pourquoi es-tu venu à Paris?'

'L'amour,' Camille said and left her lips parted as though there was a conclusion to that story and she wasn't sharing it. That's where the story or the trust between two women dried up. Which one, she wasn't sure. Back to the computer screen:

> *I'm here. Define 'moustache'.*

> *What are we dealing with? Anything wispy, sporadic or bumfluffy, get off-line and leave the room asap!*

> *No.*

> *Phew!*

*So if the man*

*(or woman – how would I know – you ARE in Europe!)…*

> *Lets assume 'man'!*

46

> *Ok (\*cough, and blush like a lady\*)*

*Ok if your man is sporting a small, neat, personable tuft, you can overlook it*

*(only if he buys you Lindt Linour)*

> *Not really …*

> *Ah – a man with the ability to grow one … snap him up before someone else does!*

*Tho, between you and me; if you meet one with that cute stubbly thing going on just under the bottom lip have a go with him too. Trust me.*

*My curry's here. I'm off. I miss you.*

*XXX PS If you find two, tell me and I'll discover Eurostar! XXX*

Zoë's world and her way were fiction now. And so, she looked at him again: there was something of a tempter in him. Those eyes were solid. And his face – the part on him where dark beard gave way to pink cheeks – it needed to be touched, tenderly, that place of transformation. And when he smiled, his cheeks raised out of their place. He was soft in there, somewhere. He smoked constantly. In theory, she didn't like this.

'I am in love with you,' he said, in English.

'No, you're not,' she said and laughed. 'You don't even know me.'

There are some men. She became weak in the mouth. She struggled. They fed each other English, in rapid, passionate gushes. They spoke about their physical reaction to certain words: *pamplemousse, ténèbres,* discombobulate, and he said he'd cook her some eggs. She declined. This was where trouble lay.

'Don't trust Gabriel,' the Door Keeper said when she rolled out of the bar that night.

'Breakfast?' he said again.

'No.'

And as they walked in no particular direction, together, street vendors smiled at him.

'I've been here forever,' he said. 'Breakfast? Go on.'

'No.'

They walked over a drain with a graffiti arm reaching out of it; over Euro coins tarmaced into the street outside a Chinese take-away. On a pavement of gold, she thought, love zaps her blood sugar. No not love, either. But it made sense of Shakespearean idiots, whatever it was. She was drunk and starving and something else. A jittery and untrustworthy love. No, no, madness. It was just silly. It was fake. It would pass.

And it was raining. If he couldn't offer her warm food, he offered her his hat, he said. This was not the act of an untrustworthy man, she thought as she smelled his hair where hers was. And back in her hotel, she lay in her bed, guilty, smelling of – not her, not her on her skin. He was there when she closed her eyes and there even more when she woke up in the dark, bent double, embracing a wall. In the morning, she thought: flat hunting, no coffee. Then she bumped into him in the street anyway. She didn't know what it was about him but he made her feel the multitudes of other selves in her, shuddering against each other. This was perfect. It was what it was. It wouldn't pass.

*

48

'I want to cook you a British breakfast. What goes into it, besides eggs?' Eggs, he had.

'Bacon, sausages, mushrooms, grilled tomatoes.'

He picked up his socks and tried putting them on while still looking at the ingredient names coming out of her lips.

'Beans, black pudding.'

'That's just weird,' he said. 'Bloody Brits and beans! We'll leave those out. Besides, we'd never find any!' And he was ready.

This is only grocery shopping, she said. They were not holding hands when it got colder in the fridge aisles. It was just a thought. It was wonderful. One day, it would only be a story; remember it.

Two people from two different places, making eggs, involved negotiation. They stepped on each other's toes in his tiny kitchen until the toes of their socks were teased off. The impossibly small space didn't faze him. He knew it well: balanced things in places she hadn't even spotted (cardboard box flap, sink corner, hip). They knocked knuckles as they met in the middle over how runny a yolk should be and if two was enough or should they make four. Mainly, she left him to it, stood back and still she was close enough to place her hands on his waist and nuzzle in his hair.

'I suppose scrambled,' he said, 'but I suppose I should ask you how you like yours. I don't know things like that about you.'

'I like them poached.'

'That would be perfect. We'll poach all of them.'

'All?'

'Sure. I'm ravenous.'

49

They also had bacon and sausage (Toulouse was the only one available) and bread (flute, not loaf) and mushrooms.

'How on earth are they supposed to be cooked?' he asked.

'Some butter is fine,' she said, but it wasn't in him to leave it at that.

'Just butter?

'Yes.'

He squirmed. 'No,' he said, 'no, it's not right.' He added garlic and green peppers and cream and then, only then, were the mushrooms mushrooms. At least she was in charge of the eggs – she showed him what poaching was, showed him how to get them out of hot water without bursting them. And this way they had, the grace of steps in a two by half metre kitchen, it scared her, scared her more than sex.

They walk back into rue Nollet together. They even look alike: couples do, don't they, after a little while? The same food: same nourishment, same poison in the light of their eyes and the sag of their jeans. When they open the café door, they both pause, see their fractured reflection in the mirror-mosaic pillar by the entrance: they are brushstrokes of light. They giggle at how they look together and walk in.

Luc sees what we see and makes a beautiful tale to tell about the two. He fills the gaps between what he sees, what he's told and what he wants for them. He thinks hard about the feelings he'll give them; a useful distraction on a slow morning at work. Jean tells him to stop mooning, stop staring into space, hello there, is he in love or something?

'Non,' and he makes coffee on autopilot.

It bothers him that he can't imagine a happy ending for them. That's just how it goes, he thinks. Then shifts the empty coffee cups around until they make a shape that pleases him.

Such a beautiful tale it is too; so beautiful, he thinks he should write it down. He never gets around to it though, and eventually the details turn a pug coffee-stained colour and he can't see them clearly any more. Instead he watches one of his locals making doodles and like that, his time goes. His stories never get finished.

*

She wondered in and out of various streets in Paris, alone, sometimes stopped, sat. Love, she decided, was stored up in her bone marrow. There, she could do nothing about it. She could layer up against the seasons but nothing more – she liked layers. Now, something about her was older than her years. She lived on baguettes so old they weren't fit to be sold and could only be bought back to life by soaking in cupfuls of coffee.

Sometimes, just sometimes, a rose seller gave her a half-dead rose. A deception or joke, she realised, but she wasn't sure which. It meant one thing: she wasn't invisible, yet. She just had to wait, she would be. She clutched her rose stalk, she mumbled for more coffee. A local cartoonist captured her once in a while. The discarded drawings were brushed into rue Nollet then rue des Dames with sugar sachets and cigarette buts. They were light and flew far.

Some people stay, some find their way out. That artist, Manet, eventually left that street for good, too. The conclusion of his love story was that he got to marry his Suzanne, as soon as his father, the Judge, was dead and gone and unable to judge. And when their friend, Degas, painted a portrait of the couple as a gift, old Manet thought it didn't flatter his beloved Suzanne as it should (was it too real or just cruel?). Manet ripped it in half. He loved her then? When they left the street, she became tolerant of his roving eye and they lived happily ever after.

# The Vegetable Beds

**Angharad Penrhyn Jones**

After I left my husband, Sam, my parents reminded me of all the reasons I should change my mind. They talked a great deal about his horticultural skills.

'Think of all the salad he grows for you!' my mother said. 'And that beautiful broccoli!' They assumed that he treated me like he treated his peas: that he was gentle, attentive, paternal as a priest.

(When my father referred to the generous dimensions of Sam's onions, I had to get up from the table. 'I've never responded well to onions,' I said, welling up. 'They have important anti-inflammatory properties,' my mother called out as I left the room.)

They also approved of my husband's occupation. If he wasn't caring for his vegetables, Sam was tending to the needs of six hundred teenagers. As a head teacher he was renowned for his campaign to encourage healthy eating in schools, and he'd established an extraordinary school allotment. My father, having worked in the police force for almost forty years, was impressed by his son-in-law's relationship with the pupils. 'Head teachers are just managers these days,' Dad used to say.

'They might as well be running football teams. But Sam's different. He cares about those kids, you can tell.'

My parents hadn't always been so sure about him. Mam had started to cough when I told them, six weeks after Sam and I first met, that we were getting engaged. She coughed for quite a long time, while Dad removed the batteries from the radio and rolled them between his fingers without saying a word.

Around two hours later, the batteries back in the radio, he said, 'He's a lot older than you, my love.'

We were an odd-looking couple, I knew that. Sam was a big man, built for rugby, and he had a shock of wavy red hair which made your heart stop when you first saw it. His freckles made him glow. At the beginning, when I stood next to him with my tiny frame and my disappointing hair – thin, the colour of ash – I could see the concern in my parents' eyes.

'You're like a mouse when you're with him,' Mam told me. 'You look so small and you go all quiet. I keep expecting you to disappear into a hole.'

But maybe she looked closer and saw a flush on my cheeks. My new boyfriend had a deft tongue: he was the only man I'd slept with who could negotiate the consonants in my name. 'Oh Esyllt,' he'd murmur as his mouth moved over my neck, my nipples, my thighs, and my whole body would break into song.

My mother is called Llinos: she knew about the importance of getting consonants right. She also understood the value of optimism. Soon she was inviting us over every week. Mam would chat to Sam about vegetable steamers and school dinners and child obesity, while Dad asked for his opinions on the

54

social services. I wouldn't contribute much. I'd just gaze at my *cariad* across the table, his forearms as chunky as salmon, hair like flames around his face, and I'd feel queasy with pride. This man was not only larger than life: he was larger than death. It was impossible to believe that anything could put out that fire.

\*

'We never see Sam these days,' Mam said a few months into our marriage, after he'd stopped coming with me to Sunday lunch. 'Do you think he objects to our supermarket carrots?' I reassured her that I didn't see much of him either. 'Well, it's understandable,' she said. 'He's under so much pressure.'

There were meetings after school and other commitments on the weekends. He'd come home from work to hoe and water the beds, to tend to the greenhouse plants and remove caterpillar eggs from the cabbages with one of my old paintbrushes. He cooked delicious meals but he usually ate them in front of the computer. And late at night, he'd emerge from his study to wage war on the slugs with a pair of scissors and a torch. While the lettuces thrived, I lay in bed and wilted.

'I miss you, Sam,' I told him on our first wedding anniversary.

He leaned across the table and stroked my cheek. 'I know, I know. It's not easy.'

'We need to spend time together,' I said. 'We need to *hang out* together. Isn't that what couples are meant to do? Or has there been some sort of terrible misunderstanding on my part?'

55

'Esyllt, *please*.'

'When was the last time we watched a film together?'

He traced my eyebrow with his index finger. 'Sometimes work has to take first priority. You know that.'

'"Sometimes work has to take first priority,"' I said flatly. I pulled away from him. 'Do you know the Latin for that? We could have it as our motto, you know, above the bed, to remind me why I'm always alone. I'll design a nice crest for us. What do you think?'

'Look, when you're running a school, you're in the firing line. If I don't—'

'Nobody's forcing you to do this work.'

'I'm good at my job.'

'I'm so pleased for you.'

He sighed. I could see him scrutinising my eyes, looking for the dark half-moons which appear before my period.

'Sam, do you still love me?'

'Of course I love you! I love you more than anything.' He grabbed my hand. 'You're the love of my life.' He said this with so much conviction that I didn't quite believe him. After a moment, he said, 'There is one thing. The smoking. You know it bothers me.'

I took a deep breath. 'I like smoking. It helps me pass the time when I'm alone.'

'Do you want to die of cancer?'

'I won't die of cancer. I eat far too much broccoli.'

We scowled at each other.

'Come on,' he said, 'let's not argue on our anniversary.' He got up from the table, placed my head against his stomach and leaned down to kiss my hair. His lips were pillowy against my scalp, his breath hot. My legs weakened. 'Come to bed,' he said, and he took my hand. He was good at resolving conflicts and this made me burn with rage.

That summer I was illustrating a children's story about animals who envy the attributes of other species. (The seagull resents the dolphin's ability to swim; the dolphin wishes he could walk sideways over sand like a crab.) I often sat out in the garden during the day; I enjoyed watching the birds while I smoked. The vegetables were interesting too. I liked the blond wispy hair sprouting from the sweetcorn, and the cos lettuces with their crinkly leaves and solid hearts. More than anything, I admired the way the peas' tendrils clung to the bamboo sticks. They put me in mind of a child's limbs wrapped around the legs of her father.

*

Four months after our anniversary, when the air was deliciously smoky and Sam was busy with leaf mould, I turned thirty. On the morning of my birthday Sam brought me a box of the organic champagne truffles he always provided on special occasions. 'You can have your present tonight,' he said. 'And I'll cook you the best meal of your life, I promise. Something with chard. And feta maybe? I'll try to be home by eight.' He kissed me briefly and left me sitting up in bed munching truffles. Then I lay down again and nuzzled my pillow, asking myself why I had chosen to marry a man whose presence in my life was defined by absence.

We had fallen in love during a train journey from Cardiff. Sam was on his way back from a conference and was tired; I'd been to an art exhibition and was disillusioned. He sat on the opposite side of the table and for a few seconds the sight of his hair stole my breath. I never really recovered from the lack of oxygen, and during the following two hours, over a terrible coffee and a thrilling conversation about therapeutic art, I overcame my shyness and began to flirt.

The train ripped through rainy market towns; people got up and sat down and shuffled along the aisle; but somehow all this happened outside our field of vision. We were travelling on our own private train: that of our mutual interests. We talked about our love of rural Wales and our antipathy towards Cardiff. We discussed our interest in foreign films and were startled to discover that, unlike everyone we knew, we had both found *Amélie* cloying. He revealed that the film had almost caused him to break up with his ex-girlfriend, who'd watched it five times and bought the soundtrack. I felt inexplicably jealous of this ex-girlfriend and shook my head at the absurdity of her behaviour. I told him that *Amélie* had put me off visiting Paris for life. When he laughed, he exposed strong, white teeth, with no sign of cavities.

We stopped at Newtown, Machynlleth, Dyfi Junction, and as we drew closer to our destination I felt my cheeks grow hot. His nose reddened. We leaned in close, our arms almost touching. Standing on the platform in Aberystwyth, watching me light up the cigarette I was desperate for, he invited me to jump in his car. 'I've got some films you might like to borrow,' he said. 'I'll take you home later.' We both knew this was a lie; but the lie was delivered so coolly, with so little effort, that there was no need for anyone to feel ashamed. In the car we stared ahead and talked about light, insubstantial subjects, as if we were saving our appetites for the main course.

His cottage, situated in a hamlet I'd never heard of, fifteen miles to the south, was whitewashed and damp and smelled of earth. It was beautiful, but it needed more textiles, more colour. Though it was too dark to see anything through the kitchen window, I could sense the vegetation growing in the back garden: a flurry of flowers and vegetables and fruit trees. 'I have fantastic soil,' he said. 'I've been building it up for years.' My nose pressed against the cold glass, I had a vision of myself sitting out there in summer, studying bees and butterflies and wide-eyed marigolds, capturing all that life with pencil and paper; and while my mind was consumed by this scenario, Sam stood behind me and put his arms around my waist as if we were husband and wife.

His bed was soft and unmade; it smelled of an unfamiliar body. And what a body! When he whispered my name as he brought me to orgasm, I decided that I never wanted to sleep anywhere else. The next morning, sipping an espresso in bed, I knew that I would abandon my bedsit, and all those ideas my mother had imposed on me about getting to know a man 'as a friend' before handing over your heart. What did mothers know about the kind of love that took over your body like a virus, the kind that hit you at a *cellular level*? Our mothers cared too much about propriety, had themselves been brainwashed by parents with one foot in the Victorian age. Within a week I had moved my stuff in. Within two weeks, I was painting the bathroom walls pumpkin-orange and giving up smoking. By the end of the month, we were choosing rings.

Sam and I had told each other this story over and over, and we'd enjoyed relating a version of these events to our families and friends. This morning, though, none of it felt real. It was a film I'd watched too many times. I got up; I needed a cigarette.

I paused outside Sam's study. The door was half-open. He was usually careful to close it, even when he was out of the house: he said it helped him to separate work from home life. I stepped inside. This was the only room in the house I hadn't attacked with a paintbrush, owing to his reluctance to let me interfere with his papers. ('I'm worried about things getting misplaced,' he'd say. 'And besides, I don't even notice the wallpaper.') I scanned the neat piles of utility bills, the carefully-labelled box files, the post-it notes with his tiny handwriting. There were no prints on the walls and the books were dull: *Behaviour Management Pocketbook, School Governors' Yearbook, Growing Your Own Fruit*. His desk was streaked with morning sun; the light beckoned me. I sat in the swivel chair and for a long time I stared at the monitor's black screen, trying not to see my own reflection.

Why did I choose my birthday to go searching for the truth about my husband? Maybe I wanted to get the whole business out of the way before moving into a new decade. Or did I have a newfound sense of entitlement, perhaps, as though I'd been handed some sort of licence with those chocolate truffles? Either way, I ignored the contractions in my gut and reached over to press the button.

One evening, back in the beginning, when Sam and I were studying stars from the bedroom window – still warm and salty from making love, still a little drunk from the wine – Sam had told me that he used the names of constellations for his internet passwords. I'd felt a welling in my throat as he chanted those words into the night. What a man he was! What a poet!

I scanned Wikipedia for constellations and got his password on the fifteenth attempt: Ophiuchus.

It didn't take long to find the evidence. Even now, I can remember the sound of the cry in the toilet bowl; the taste of chocolate and bile.

\*

I told Sam I knew he was having sex with someone at work. A teaching assistant, barely out of college, with exquisite breasts – as firm as cabbages – and a fondness for the camera. 'I suppose you've been using your office,' I said. 'And I suppose she's not your first.' He didn't deny it, but he denied its significance. He begged me to stay. He begged me to stay quiet. It was the first time I'd seen him cry.

'I don't want anyone to find out about this,' he said, fighting for breath. 'You know what the governors are like, they wouldn't—'

'You think I should protect you? That I should be your shield?'

I was speaking to his feet; I couldn't look into those bloodshot eyes.

'Please,' he said. 'Don't—'

'I'd rather be a human shield in the Gaza Strip,' I said, and later that night I packed a suitcase and left.

*

My paintings became, in my mother's words, 'a bit impenetrable'. I had taken over their conservatory and one searingly cold morning in November she came in to watch me paint. She inspected the twelve canvasses lined up side by side.

'So what are you working on here?' she asked.

'They're abstract,' I said. 'Red over white.'

'Yes, I can see that. So is this a "spot the difference" exercise?'

I refused to return the smile.

'Listen to me, *cariad*,' she said. She positioned herself in front of the heater. 'You can't just give up on him like this. I mean, most men are bloody difficult to live with – not that I'm going to talk about your father here.' She rubbed her eyes; she seemed tired. 'Believe me, a marriage can never be perfect, just like a painting can never turn out exactly as you hope. Are you listening?'

'Uh-huh.' I stood back to scrutinise my work.

'It's painful, but that's how life is. In the end you have to commit to things. You have to cope with a bit of … ugliness.'

'I don't think—'

'I know it's not easy for an artist, and you've always been a perfectionist. But there's no point chasing the horizon, is there? You have to work with what's in front of you.'

'Are we talking about Sam here? Or about art? I'm confused'

'You know what I'm talking about. I'm talking about your tendency to be disappointed by things. By yourself, by your work, by other people. You have to learn to get over those frustrations. And the other thing, men need a lot of attention. If they don't get it, things start to go wrong.'

The three woolly jumpers I'd put on that morning made me feel big and powerful. I lifted my arm behind my shoulder and flicked the brush. Red paint splattered against glass. Mam drew a sharp breath and stared at me with a hand on her mouth. I barged out to the garden to have a smoke.

After many hours had passed, slow and dark as tar, she walked into the spare room and offered me her arms. She smelled of my childhood, and I clenched my fists to stop the tears.

'I just don't want you to do anything you'll end up regretting,' she said quietly.

Then she hissed at my father in their bedroom; I could hear his silence through the wall.

In the mirror I saw a child, hollow-cheeked, her eyes distant. I couldn't bear to look at her. I went downstairs to watch a romantic comedy and waited for the dénouement. Finally it came: the couple turned to face each other under a beech tree and started to kiss, the symphony building up to its crescendo like a woman reaching orgasm, violin strings quivering with pleasure.

I was cold. I switched off the television and covered my legs with a blanket that smelled of our old dog, long dead. It made my legs itch. I scratched and scratched. I chewed the inside of my cheeks. Then I walked upstairs, still shivering, and knocked on my parents' door.

\*

These days, Sam gets his vegetables from the supermarket. In June I went to visit him, when the sun was high and hostile in the Manchester sky. His kitchen had a view of a concrete yard, north-facing. Under the strip-lights his skin was the colour of cement, the freckles like a symptom of a rare disease. He'd shaved his head, and his scalp was dusted with embers as if he'd been released from hell.

'You look different,' I said.

'You too.'

He was studying me across the table. His eyes were lifeless, the pupils small like seeds. Somewhere in the distance I heard a police siren. I swallowed hard.

'So, what's the new school like?' I asked.

'I start in September.' He sighed. 'It's going to be tough.'

'You always liked a challenge.'

He turned to face the window.

I focused on my breathing. 'Actually I'm here to talk about the house. My solicitor said—'

'I don't … want to discuss the practicalities.' His speech was a little slurred. 'I just …'

He stopped talking. For a while we stared at each other.

'Sam, are you on some sort of … medication?'

'I'm on every sort of medication.'

I opened my mouth but there was something stuck in my throat. I started to cough. He was biting his nails; I'd never seen them this clean. I glanced down at his shoes and pictured the toes curled up inside them. They were the only part of him I felt I knew.

'Esyllt,' he said.

I looked up at him. In my ears I heard the thrum of blood.

'Make use of the garden,' he said. 'The peas should be ready now. Cook them straight away, before the sugars break down. Leave them too long and they'll turn to starch.'

I said nothing.

'And the lettuce needs harvesting too,' he said. 'Don't let it go to waste.'

*

The garden was a wilderness by the time I returned. The leeks had mutated into giant ornamental flowers, with seedheads like pompoms balancing on long stalks; and the lettuces had turned into miniature conical trees. I did a few sketchings: bolted plants have an unpredictable beauty.

Now that we're having this dry weather, I've been coming to the garden most days. I've ripped my arms to shreds tackling the bramble, but it's satisfying work, and there's a lot to be done before I phone the estate agent.

As I tug at the weeds, a robin bobs around, waiting for worms. 'Come closer,' I say. 'I won't hurt you.' He looks me straight in the eye and takes off.

# Welsh Gold

## Francesca Rhydderch

Friday nights were always the worst. By ten o'clock the punters were getting leery, trying to catch her eye as she handed them their change.

'Sharpen up a bit,' said Steve behind her. 'There's people waiting.'

She dropped the wet, dirty coins into the open palm stretched out in front of her, slammed the till shut and swung round to serve the next customer.

'What can I get you?' she said.

She knew straightaway that he was a traveller. She'd seen the trailers down by the river, and clothes hung up to dry on makeshift washing lines. They came with the fair in winter, but in the summer they just brought their vans and set up camp while the farms were on the look-out for fruit pickers.

'Double whisky,' he said, reaching into his back pocket for his wallet, and then, 'I know you, don't I?'

She did remember him, come to think of it, taking money for the rides at the Christmas fair, his eyes glittering down at her, stuck in a dodgem with Mike, who'd had a few and insisted on ramming into all and sundry, even the kids.

'This one's broken, mate, you'll have to get off,' he'd said, and Mike, not having the upper hand for once, had been in a foul mood for the rest of the night.

She nodded and turned away towards the optic.

'Penderyn good enough for you?'

'It'll do,' he said. She could hear the smile in his voice.

'Make that two,' said another voice.

'You don't know what he's having yet,' she said over her shoulder, surprising herself. She never joked with customers. Steve said she was a miserable cow.

'I know what he's having.'

Both men laughed as she put their drinks on the bar, and she saw they were brothers, although the one who'd just come in had a deep frown line down the middle of his tanned forehead, and flecks of grey in his hair. They wore gold, lots of it, expensive watches and chunky signet rings on their little fingers.

'You keep your eyes to yourself, Nathan,' said the older one, winking at Mona.

'Shut up, Terry,' said Nathan. 'I thought I knew her, that's all.'

'You're not bloody duckering again like a woman, are you?'

The younger one downed his drink with a grin on his face.

Mona wanted to stay where she was, her arms folded on the bar, listening to them trade jibes for her entertainment while she waited for her next order, but she could see Steve keeping an eye on her from the lounge.

'Come and see to this lot while I go down the cellar,' he shouted over to her. As she went through the open doorway she could still feel the reel and tug of the brothers' warm voices behind her.

The drinkers' talk in the lounge was cushioned by plush velveteen chair backs and people in smart clothes who ordered gin and tonics and watched breaking news on the telly. Posh types, who didn't have much to say to her, and didn't tell her to have a drink herself when they handed over their twenty-pound notes. Mona didn't mind, though. She liked working on her own, without Steve getting at her all the time. Although he was always giving her stick, she wasn't bad at her job. She was a bit timid, perhaps, her voice flimsy and not really up to calling for last orders or badgering the slackers to get going, but she could hold a tray of full pint glasses with one hand and a slew of empties in the other. She didn't drop spirit measures or give people the wrong change. But by the time Steve came back up from the cellar one of the pumps was broken and another one was leaking. Each time she tried to pull a pint the tap sprayed warm beer over her.

'Can't trust you to do anything, can I?' Steve said, rolling a keg in under one foot. 'What the hell have you gone and done now?'

Mona tried to ignore him. She tilted the half-pint glass she was holding, watching the beer cream up to the top. He wasn't going to let things rest, though. He came up and put his wrinkled face close to hers, too close. 'It's them gypos, innit?' he said. 'I bet your old man would want to know how you're tarting yourself about.'

'He's your boss, remember,' she said quietly.

69

Nathan and Terry were still sitting at the other bar. Nathan was looking straight at her. Under the lights she could see how pale his skin must be under the sunburn, and the dark shadows under his eyes. She reached for a fresh glass from the shelf behind Steve.

'Yours and all.' Steve spat the words out, turning round and bending down as she did, keeping his mouth close to her ear. He straightened up and elbowed his way through the packets of crisps hanging off the doorway leading back into the bar. He leaned towards Nathan and Terry, talking too quietly for her to hear him. They didn't rise to whatever vicious bait he was feeding them. They got up in silence, almost dignified, and put their empties on the bar. Terry glanced over at her, but it was Nathan she gawped at, not caring what Steve thought. Then they were gone. The ice cubes in their shot glasses hadn't even melted into the dregs of whisky.

It was a Friday night, wasn't it? She shouldn't have thought this one would turn out any different. She was glad of the peace when stop-tap came, and she could be quiet in herself, with only the hum of the beer chiller cutting through the silence. She stacked and emptied the glass washer over and over, until all the shelves were full to the front again. She took her time, trying to put off the moment when Steve would lock up and she would walk home along the prom and let herself in, calling out 'Hello?' as she always did, but not expecting an answer, because Mike would be comatose on the sofa in front of the telly with the sound down, one of his soft porn channels throwing shadow puppets over the takeaway cartons on the coffee table.

She tipped the chairs onto their front legs against the tables ready for the cleaner to get round with the hoover in the morning. She put a hand on the back of the high bar stool where Nathan had been sitting, and ran her fingers along the polished wood. She pulled herself up on it and took a breather while she waited for Steve to finish counting up.

'Give my regards to your old man,' he said, finally, handing over her wages.

'Will do.' She didn't know why he always said that. There didn't seem to be much love lost between him and Mike.

She nudged her way past him to the low sink behind the bar where she kept a pot of hand cream and her wedding ring in a clean glass.

It was gone. The glass was still there, leaning in against the hot tap, but it was empty. The hoop of Welsh gold had disappeared.

'It's not there,' she said. 'My ring's gone.'

Steve didn't call her a dozy bitch, or laugh and tell her that her old man would have something to say if she went home without it. He worked his way round the shelves under the bar looking for it, taking glasses and bottles out and slotting them back in face out. He looked under all the settles and pulled cushions up from the sofas in the corner.

'That little gypo bastard,' he said, pulling his hand out of the seam of one of the old settees by the door. He held the ring up to the light. 'He must have nicked it and then slipped it down here on his way out. Spiteful little tyke.'

Mona put her hand out and took the ring. Steve took a cigarette out of his shirt pocket and put it in his mouth.

'I'll get 'em for this.'

'No, don't,' said Mona. 'It must have been a mistake. It couldn't have been him.'

But Steve was out the door already. She followed him onto the square. He went through town past the Llew Du to the cut-price supermarkets by the river. She used to love coming to the mart on a Wednesday with her father; the smell of the penned-in animals, and the men bunched around them, farmers with big hands who spoke only to agree a sale. Now there was a pet food shop where her father used to sell his lambs in spring, their breath steaming out into the morning air.

It was her father she missed the most. Not the farm at the top of the mountain, or the lake with the buzzards circling above it.

It was easy to keep up with Steve, although he seemed to know his way well enough, pushing his hands through the knotweed that had grown across the towpath. The water was low and smelled bad, but there was no getting away from it. The path clung to the riverbank past the football field and the industrial estate, until the base of the valley flattened out and the trees opened up to the black sky.

As they got closer to the campsite, she thought the travellers must be packing up: there were lights on and some of the trailers had been moved. Vans were parked in a ring so their headlights shone onto a circle of cobbled earth. A group of men was gathered around the space in the middle. A small boy sat on a gas cylinder turned on its side.

'Fight,' said Steve under his breath.

'What?'

The fights Mona knew were the skirmishes that broke out in the pub before closing time, when offence was taken for no reason, and arms and legs went flying and kicking all over the place until the disagreement was sealed with fists on the pavement outside. This was different. There was a man standing apart, looking at his watch. He tapped it with a tattooed finger and glanced around him.

'Ready?' he said.

Two men stepped out of the crowd.

'Yes,' said Terry. He nodded over at Nathan. 'We're ready.'

'Remember to fight fair, now,' said the man. 'No kicking and no biting.'

Terry nodded impatiently. Nathan looked frightened.

'Come on, mush,' Terry shouted. 'Get rid of your gansey.'

Nathan pulled his jumper off. His bare chest shone and shook in the glare of the lights.

Terry pulled his own top off carelessly with one hand, and flung it away. It landed in the dried mud by her feet and a Jack Russell next to her barked sharply. The man with the watch said something she couldn't catch, and Terry and Nathan walked towards each other.

Once they were almost toe to toe, they took a step back. They circled around each other for a while; fists raised, feet skipping from side to side.

The dog barked again. Panicked, Nathan lunged out skittishly. His bare knuckles hit the side of Terry's head with a crack, and Terry roared. He pummelled Nathan in the chest and then the head, over and over again. He uncoiled a right hook, then a left, right, left, right, until Nathan was staggering, his fists crunched up around his head.

Terry sent out two straight punches. Blood sputtered out of Nathan's ear and dribbled down his neck and back. His face was creased up, his eyes pressed shut. Terry flicked a jab to the other side of his head, then grabbed him with one arm, holding him by the neck and swinging him round. He threw him to the floor.

'Kushtie, Terry,' said the referee.

Nathan lay on the ground like a limp trout on the riverbank.

Terry put an arm out and Nathan pulled himself up on it.

'That'll teach you, you thieving, stinking pikie,' said Steve.

Terry turned. He took them in, Steve and her, standing there in the headlights. 'Go home,' he said.

Steve turned and went, but Mona stood her ground. The blood was starting to dry on Terry's face and hands, so that it looked like mud. The whites of his eyes glistened. He lifted one blood-caked hand to his cheek and rubbed it, putting his other arm round Nathan's shoulders.

'Go home, I said.' Terry's voice was louder this time.

'Not yet.' Mona spoke loudly too, but she was scared. She half-expected him to come over and slap her across the face, but he didn't.

'All right,' he said.

She held Nathan's other arm and helped Terry get him to his van. They staggered back and fore as if they were on a three-legged pub crawl. She felt Nathan's hard ribs pressing against her breasts through her beer-stained top, and breathed in the smell of sweat mixed with blood, and something else too as they clambered up the metal steps into the pitch black of the caravan. It was the scent of over ripe strawberries silted up under his fingernails.

He flung himself onto an unmade bed and an empty coffee cup rolled off the blanket and hit the floor. She picked it up, slipped her ring into it, and slid it under the bed for safekeeping.

The travellers didn't come back, not that winter for the fair, nor the summer after that. Mona went walking on hot afternoons down to the triangle of field where they'd camped, and sat in the long grass where no one would see her. As she walked back into town, watching the fog coming in from the bay, she held her baby tight in to her chest, her hand shading the crown of his head from the rain.

People stopped her on the street to get a look at him.

'Looks like Mike, doesn't he?' they said, stroking his hop-coloured hair.

She nodded, stepping aside as a couple of boys pushed past her on the narrow pavement. The slate slabs underfoot were wet and slippery, and she almost lost her balance. She put a hand out to a stretch of iron railings to steady herself.

'He's his father's son, all right,' she said.

# The Parrot House

**Zillah Bethell**

*I need a woman who can cut pencils and make puddings.*
From the letters of Edward Lear.

## I. The Jumbly Girl

Dear Em,

You ask me to describe him. Well, he's as tall as a giraffe on stilts with an elephantine nose (his words) and periwinkle eyes behind a pair of wire spectacles. His *tout ensemble* is one of supremely awkward grace. He has a capacious mouth full of silly puns and nonsense rhymes (the inconvenient children, he calls them, liable to leapfrog into his mind when he's on the verge of sliding into the arms of Morpheus or at some other inopportune moment); and *extremely* capacious pockets containing (as God is my witness) two alpine plants, a Claude glass, sunflower seeds for Adelphi (more on whom later), one hard-boiled egg wrapped up in a handkerchief, a teasel for combing his hair when he is on the move, and a little white mouse with lemony eyes, raspberry ears and a heart the size of a peachstone – Adelphi. He is quite adorable. The mouse I mean, though Mr. Lear is not entirely disagreeable himself. Oh Em, surely father could not disapprove of a man who is friends with Mr. Tennyson? Edward intends to set some of his poems to music – he is particularly fond of *Mariana*. He is a fine musician as well as an artist. By the by, did you find the sheet music for *Faerie Voices* you were after? Edward says he meets a multitude of young ladies who can play fantasias on the pianoforte but do not have the wherewithal to make a crumble; and succumb to the vapours at the bat of a grasshopper's eyelash. As you know, I have never suffered from the vapours so I remarked in as stout a tone as I could muster, 'Hartshorn or Asafoetida applied to the nose should dispel the vapours in most cases. If further measures need to be taken, a lit feather brought close to the crinolines will hardly fail to induce the afflicted young lady out of her vapourish realm.'

He seemed vastly amused by that and said that perhaps at last he had found a sturdy rock to barnacle his boots to. We ate with relish the hamper Cook prepared for us. Mr Lear declared it was heavenish 'scent'.

*Your cook is a veritable dish*, he sang,
*Leg of mutton, mulberry jam*
*And buttercups fried with fish.*

Needless to say, we had nothing of the kind. In truth we ate beef pastries, frangipanis (how I love Cook's frangipanis), elderflower cordial and aniseed bread which Edward deemed must forever after be termed 'apostrophe bread' because the tiny seeds look like apostrophes. Then he said he had a very important question to ask me. You may imagine the colour fled my face as Wilson puts it. Here I am, thought I, on a bench in the dwarf shrubbery of Marylebone Park, and am about to be asked a very important question.

'We are in some romantic, classical land,' he began (he is most awfully fond of romantic, classical lands), 'like Troy or Athens, by the Hellespont, Parnassus.'

'Yes.' I barely breathed it.

'We are down to our last crumb of apostrophe bread and to stave off morbidious starvation we are offered parrot or rabbit pie. Which, my dear Gussie, do you choose?'

I found it hard to collect my thoughts at this point, they had flown so high, but in the end I said it could not be rabbit on account of fond recollections of a childhood pet (dear little Nibbles); he on the other hand, could not say parrot for upon that noble family of *psittacidæ* depended his livelihood, having been born without inheritance, brains, looks or charm.

'You may have been born without an inheritance,' I remonstrated, 'but on the last three points you are quite unjust.'

Was I too forward? Sometimes I do not know if I am too forward, too backward, too stout, too prim, too proud, too reckless. How to be in the company of a man? He did not appear offended but my cheeks boiled like the sun and I was glad to unpin my veil and eclipse them in a cloud of lace. Luckily a distraction arrived – a young boy on his way to visit the diorama. Edward quite cheered up at the sight of him and took great pains to entertain him with Adelphi, setting him in the palm of his hand with some sunflower seeds; and showing him his Claude glass. We all took a peek at the view reflected in the small black convex mirror – marmalade coloured tulips from Amsterdam, the size of fingernails; the lake, equal in magnitude to the Serpentine, reduced to a dewdrop; and Wilson in miniature on her campstool with my watercolour caddy at her side, a hand across her eyes as if in mild reproach at the sun. Or me. By the by, she mentions sassafras shavings for bugs. You see, I am collecting domestic receipts for when my turn comes. If it ever does. Oh Em, am I to count linen and keep a tally of glass and plate for the rest of my life just for father?

Mr. Lear took his leave quite abruptly. He had an appointment with a young lady named Natalie. Should I be jealous? I do not know how to read him. Sometimes I think there is more gravity in his jokes than in him. And I am tormented by the thought that I should have chosen rabbit pie. Please write.

Your loving sister, Gussie.

## II. Multipeoplea Upsidownia

I pause by the lime green metal dome of the monkey house, shake Zephaniah's hand through the bars. He grins, asks for a banana. I shake my head sorrowfully. It is futile though. I know he knows that I will whistle Fur Coat, that Fur Coat will stagger out of the storeroom with a seagrass basket of bananas, some of them ripe, some green. Zephaniah favours the unripe, the unready, as I do. He even hums nonchalantly as the charade plays out. I whistle, Fur Coat staggers out, I signal (Fur Coat is partially deaf) one banana, no two. I don't know why we do it but we do. Performed once we perform it again and again like some ancient Chinese tea drinking ceremony. Out of habit; sheer exuberance with the formalities of existence; fear. Fear of the alternative to playing it out: the chaos, the emptiness. Or perhaps I am over-dramatising the situation. Perhaps it is simply out of kindliness to a primate.

'Fruit cake?' Fur Coat taps the tin his wife deposits in the storeroom each week like a cheque. The cakes come in a peculiar array of signatures. After a while they bounce.

'No thank you. Full to the brimming with.'

'Right you are, sir. Still on the brochure?'

He knows I am. Staring down at the sheaf of papers on my desk, I feel a headache coming on. Hope it's nothing more. I still have the ulcer on my tongue from last time, chafe it against the back of my front teeth. 'I am employed by the Zoological society to paint parrots (in reality I paint any animal they care to shove at me including the greater horseshoe bat as well as the whiptail wallaby) but I am not here to check the bro-shore for the auction of duplicate specimens. Time is pressing at my temples as we speak, narrowing them even further methinks. Funds are running low, monthly charges for colourist and printer are becoming disagreeable, nay insupportable. I am to produce fourteen folios by January. I am on my tenth lithographic plate out of a grand total of forty-two. I mustn't be distracted by bro-shores.'

'Every star has roots, sir, and every star is a soul.'

'Yes, thank you.' Fur Coat's a lively sprite. Something of a poet in fact. Beneath the claw-paw-beak-n-hoof-scarred exterior of the zoo keeper is a hungry muse. When he uses the water closet with wild abandon and the stench is worse than the hyena house after a liver-and-kidney Tuesday, I imagine his soul a Cassiopeia with tendrils reaching down into his abdomen, his groin, his bowels. Sometimes it helps. Sometimes the thought is of no service whatsoever.

*Sold at auction by Messrs Rushworth and Jarvis, Zoological Gardens, Regents Park*
　　*A pair of noble Wapati deer.*
　　On what grounds are they noble? On whose grounds?
　　*Leg bone of a moa.*

Immediately we have a problem. Who knows what a moa is? (*Explanation needed*, I jot down. *Flightless bird of New Zealand. Extinct.*) The auctions are usually attended by the landed gentry looking to add artefacts to their pseudo-scientific libraries, collect live animals for their private menageries. It is not uncommon, indeed quite *à la mode* to share crumpets at elevenses with an ace of peacocks, find a wild hog in the bog garden, meet a zebra in the middle of a croquet match causing much consternation and delight amongst the frumps, the dowagers and the debutantes. I feel the usual mix of self-pity, resentment and gratitude bubbling in the cauldron of my mind. Hope it's nothing more than a headache. These people

81

are my friends, my patrons even. So why do I question their right to tether these exotics?

'Fur Coat.'

'Yes.' He's colour-coding the moth cocoons that hang from the ceiling in an old mosquito net. Some hump and squat like small dark turds, others dangle and play the light, delicate as shell earrings.

'Would your wife know what a moa was?'

'Who?'

'Your wife. Would she know what a moa was?'

'Quite in the doldrums. I'm thinking of giving him an extra portion of suet tonight. Possibly a cuttlefish.'

As I say, Fur Coat is partially deaf, though for some time now I've had a strange inkling that this distended auditory nerve he suffers with (like Beethoven) is in actual fact a distended bilious vein he lets flow now and then in the direction of his wife for his own private amusement.

'Titania's about to pop.'

'Titania's Fritillary? Let me see.'

'Look at that. No way is she a moth. Maybe not even a fritillary. *Sui generis* she is.'

I watch the cocoon, grey and opaque as an ancient hieroglyph, convulsing frantically on a twig; and massage the back of my head cautiously. Something desperately wants to get out.

'You can never quite tell what they're going to be until they emerge, they disguise themselves so well.' He sounds like an expectant father awaiting the arrival of his firstborn. He's name-tagged them all, at least the ones he knows: Emperor, Hawk, Luna, Titania … It's a perk of the job, the discarded, damaged plant and insect specimens that arrive in the storeroom to be coaxed to breathe, bloom, moult, pop in his warm enveloping hands. I bring out of my pocket the plants I've been keeping for him.

'Switzerland?'

'Probably.'

He slips them into his Wardian case, sealing them into their own world, sealing them off from ours.

Holding our noses we venture down East Tunnel, past Raven's Aviary and the hyenas – thank goodness it's Monday – to the house of a thousand fishwives.

*We fear for our lives*
*Said the man from St. Ives*
*In the house of a thousand fishwives.*

I bring out the teasel head and comb my hair as surreptitiously as I can. I'm a vain pompossum of a man.

'Is that for Nat?' Fur Coat grins.

'No, my audience. See them gather as we speak – like a swarm of locust eaters – to ogle the latest inhabitant of the zoo. My God, they'll be throwing nuts and squashed fruit at me next.'

We creep through the side entrance of the parrot house, disturbing Constance the salmon-crested cockatoo in her sleep. She squawks, sets all the other beaks off – clackety clack clackety clack – until the whole zoo's at backgammon. Fur Coat grabs Natalie, bribes her out onto her perch with a seed cake in his leather-gloved hand. She chortles. I chortle back and settle myself on the tree trunk, drawing block on my knees, ten pencils at the ready.

'Who are you then?' A bonneted old lady enquires through the bars.

'An ornithological draughtsman, madam, here to paint the family of *psittacidæ* – for Her Majesty the Queen.' Nine times out of ten they're stunned by ornithological draughtsman. The tenth shuts up by family of *psittacidæ*. This one must be the eleventh.

'And what's that you're drawing?'

She's spotted me warming my fingers up on a sketch of an apple with a purple bonnet and pinched features remarkably similar to her own. 'The Norfolk Biffin, ma'am. Very round in circumference, knobbly in parts but not unwholesome. Chuck enough of 'em at a doctor and he'll stay away for a month.'

Natalie revolves slowly like the hands of a clock sped up. What does she see through that proud, haughty eye of hers? A foxglove, a sapling, multipeoplea upsidownia? I sketch rapidly while Fur Coat holds her steady: the crimson shriek, the chasuble wing, the dart, the swoop, the curious regard. I paint the living, moving, screaming bird unlike Audubon who draws decaying carcasses or ghoulish Gould who stuffs them senseless with their own plumes. They paint dead stars without roots. I paint birds with tendrils up to Cassiopeia.

A boy in a sailor suit with the emerald hands of a dyer's apprentice salivates at Nat's seed cake. I feel for the hard-boiled egg in my trouser pocket, warm as though fresh laid.

'My pet mouse has been using this for a pillow but it's yours if you want it.' He swallows it whole like a snake then leapfrogs into my mind unbidden.

*There was a young parrot called Natalie*
*Who desperately craved immortality*
*Now she prinks and she prinks*
*In feathers and ink*
*In the pages of Lear's Anatomy.*

'Don't look now,' Fur Coat whispers. 'Three o'clock.'

Naturally I do. Holding their noses the Messrs Rushworth and Jarvis approaching. I anticipate the conversation. I don't know why I do it but I do. A feeble flirtation with etiquette perhaps. An attempt to get a leg over social intercourse.

– Good day, Mr. Lear. Have you concluded your little sketch of *macrocercus aracanga*?

– Not quite.

– And the bro-shore?

– Not quite.

A wave softly breaks upon the shingle in my head. Oh to be faraway in an unfettered land. The horses I would stirrup, the pancake landscapes I would syrup over in a runcible spoon … The charade plays out as charades always do.

'Good day Mr. Lear.' Still holding their noses. 'Is this your study of the red and yellow macaw?' (Not as educated as they should be.)

'Yes.'

'Delightful. It is nearly finished?'

'Very nearly.'

'And the brochure?'

'Very nearly.'

The shingle slips away from me. I cannot keep my footing. This is something more than a headache. My soul migrates, inhabits the body of a passing gull, flies over this egregion of a man on the jingly shingly shore, stumbling, stumbling for evermore.

## III. The Daddy Long Legs and the Fly

The moon had struck. Fireflies were out, decorating the night. Edward's gait was already lopsided as he let himself into his rooms on Upper North Place, almost throwing Adelphi into his run, the millet sticks falling like spillikins from his trembling hands. There wasn't much time. His arms and legs could do some damage if he wasn't very careful. On the last occasion his right foot had extended out of the window and all the way down to Mr. Foy in the basement. What must he have thought? Toes tapping at his window display of geraniums.

Drugs, callisthenics, Marsala. That was the order of things. He reached for the dose of phenobarbitone he kept hidden in the tea tin, swallowed hard before his Adam's apple got the better of him; then proceeded to torture his ungainly body in a set of rigorous exercises: starfish, hoop, hopscotch, flutter kick. Starfish, hoop, hopscotch, flutter kick. Until he began to sweat. Starfish, hoop, hopscotch, flutter kick. Once or twice he'd managed to sweat out the demon. Starfish, hoop, hopscotch, flutter kick. But not tonight. The demon actively licked the salt on his skin in delight. Edward blinked. His left foot had just gone up a shoe size. Soon persimmons would burst on his tongue, the sound of ticker-taping crickets in his ear. After that it wouldn't be long. Half an hour at most.

He sat at his desk, poured a glass of Marsala and inspected Fowler's china head. His landlady used old Yorick as a paperweight and it amused him to think that unpaid bills, seed packets, calling cards and correspondence were kept beneath propensities for destructiveness, amativeness and ideality.

A small white envelope, lavender scented, lay slightly apart from the rest. He opened it quickly before his eyesight failed him. The note was short, succinct, painful to him. He read it twice, sighing and tracing the sturdy, upright characters with a short, delicate finger. He felt the bumps on his own skull: ideality at the temples, the quest for immortal beauty narrowing by the minute; destructiveness above the ears, over-developed almost convex in shape; and amativeness, sexual desire at the back of the head, a dumb-bell of a bulge. Edward opened his diary and marked a cross by the day's date. *Abstinence makes no difference. I have exerted self-control for three whole weeks and still the demon visits. How can I inflict this on so sweet, so innocent a nature?*

Ironic that St. Valentine was the patron saint of epilepsy sufferers. Ironic that Hippocrates had called it the sacred disease – it was profanity in the extremity. There was no refuge in the knowledge that Julius Caesar had suffered, that Lord Byron had been a martyr to it. Had they heard the sound of cicadas before an attack? Tasted bad lemons and burnt toffee? Had they let their tongue down to their groin then rolled it back up lasciviously? On one occasion Edward's tongue had extended out of the window and all the way down to Mr. Foy in the basement. What can he have thought? A tongue licking the aphids off his window display of carnations.

There were preparations to make – a space to be cleared on the floor, a cushion, a blanket, a bucket for the nausea that often ensued, the bottle of Marsala and a plate of figs for if he woke depressed and morbidiously close to starvation. Who knew how long he'd be out for? He fitted the mouth guard, adjusting the straps under his chin. It was not unlike the one they'd used on Zephaniah for a while when they thought he'd contracted rabies. It made him look a little sinister. Edward only hoped his landlady wouldn't call in for the rent.

He unhooked his wire spectacles for they were no use now. The moon loomed large and vacant at the window. As a child he'd imagined it a flat gold disc, a coin in the pocket of heaven; as an adult he'd viewed it through the eye of a telescope, seen its cratered face, the Sea of Cold, the Sea of Crises ... The persimmons came suddenly like a woman on his tongue, the crickets chorused the state of the market on their ticker-tape machines: stock's up, stock's down. Adelphi screeched, 'I am weary, Mr. Tennyson, this life is dreary.' It seemed to Edward at that point that all life – every leaf, wing, song, heart – was on the verge of. Achingly, tremulously, regretfully on the verge of a new moment, a metamorphosis, a death.

He lay down on the floor. One Edward Lear, duplicate specimen, fit for the bro-shore. Boys in blue sailor suits with emerald hands rode the carousel of his mind, the dapple grey shades.

*There was a young gal from Westminster*
*Who nearly became an old spinster…*

He would keep that small white envelope, lavender scented, beneath the propensity for ideality, the quest for immortal beauty. Until his life concluded him. Until his soul, a sweetmeat, was taken by hyenas. On a Tuesday.

The demon set to work with his toasting fork. One Edward Lear, soon to be stuffed. Natalie, Constance, Dulcie and Emily – perched on the empty chairs of 38 Upper North Place, their tail feathers glossy with gum arabic and egg white – surveyed the convulsing object, grey and opaque, with a curious regard. Its hands punched, grabbed, shook, did the butterfly stroke. Its head banged fruitlessly at battledore and shuttlecock causing more bumps and bulges than Fowler ever depicted. And its legs – the parrots gazed in dismay – its legs bent back, cracked, hurtled the air, pedalled a bone rattler over the Alps. There was blood, urine, excrement.

*'If we were to end up in some romantic, classical land, I should*
*choose rabbit pie, Edward.*
*Always.*
Augusta.'

*One leg bone of a Lear.*
(*Explanation needed.* Who knew what a Lear was? *Flightless egregion. Extinct.*)

# The Jiltmaker

## Sarah Todd Taylor

Every bride is beautiful. In this business you have to believe that. Even the ones with buck teeth and bad hair, the fat ones and the ones who've overdone the sunbed. It doesn't matter what nature gave them, a bride must always be beautiful.

That's where I come in.

I like to think of myself as a fairy godmother. I can pluck a dress off a rail, add a few well chosen accessories and the most dowdy duckling becomes a shimmering swan. They just have to trust me. If a girl puts herself entirely in my hands, then I can almost guarantee that on her wedding day her husband won't be able to take his eyes off her. Double-take guaranteed is what I tell them.

And I like to think I'm good. In this trade you don't really want repeat business, but I get a lot of word of mouth. Bridesmaids coming back for their own weddings, that sort of thing. So I have two rules – always be nice to the bridesmaids, but always make sure the bride looks better. They come back. They know I can make them look stunning.

The thing is, when you spend most of your life trying to make silk purses out of cows' ears, it's a rare treat when you get to try out your skills on a real beauty. So when she walked into the shop that Saturday, I knew something special was about to happen.

It was coming up to closing time. She hadn't booked, just walked in and started to browse along the rail that I always keep at the front of the shop. I call it 'the icebreaker'. It gives the girls something to look at as they pluck up the courage to ask for a bit of help. I always leave them there for a while, it gives me a chance to size them up a bit, think about whether I've got anything in stock that will suit. Sad to say, some take a bit longer than others.

The first thing I noticed was her hair, dark tendrils curling round the nape of her neck and tumbling across slender shoulders. One long curl fell down in front of her collarbone, where she idly twirled it round her fingers, the other hand (such beautiful hands) pushing the dresses on the icebreaker aside one by one.

She was wearing one of those hippy skirts. The ones with little bells on cords down the front. Dreadful things – those elasticated waists should be banned. Even so, she looked slim in it. Beautifully proportioned hips, quite an elongated hourglass. She could have worn anything and looked stunning. She was perfect, the ideal model. What a shame she hadn't chosen something that would really show off her figure.

She was tall, but not so tall that I wouldn't be able to put her in heels. That's always good. Heels make a bride lean back slightly so the dress sways as she walks. You have to let the fabric live. It has to move, fold, swish. I had a bride once who put a stiff sash on a chiffon empire line. Ruined the fluidity in one baby pink stroke. Tragic.

'Let me know if you would like some help,' I said.

She glanced up and nodded, smiling. Dear goodness, that face. That smile. She was breathtaking. She looked as though she had been lovingly painted by one of the old masters, every part of her features designed and placed carefully for maximum impact. Eyes made just a little too large, mouth just a little too small, cheeks slightly flushed against a powdery cream complexion.

And then she spoke. A soft, whispery, musical voice caressing every bell-like consonant and feathery vowel.

'I'm looking for something … special.'

Every bride wants something special. Usually I can rustle something up, even for the choosiest girl. Last year I managed to adapt a red silk ballgown into a Queen of Hearts concoction, complete with crown and sceptre. Then there was the zombie bride, all red paint and torn lace. Everyone wants to be special. Sadly most only manage different.

And here was this vision asking me for something special for her. I looked at her, at her loveliness and her perfection and her exquisite beauty and I said what I say to all my girls.

'I'm sure I have just the right dress. Let's take a look on the rails, shall we.'

She tried on dress after dress. Empires, princess-lines, ballgowns, asymmetrics, everything. And she looked like a goddess in each and every one of them. I was right. She could wear anything. The empire-lines made her willowy frame look fragile and ethereal. The princess-lines and ballgowns nipped in her tiny waist and the asymmetrics made her dramatic and darkly elegant. The ivories and creams highlighted her peachy complexion. The whites, usually so hard to wear, on her were angelic. The red gown I persuaded her to try on was so striking against her dark curls that I thought I would never again see anything so beautiful.

I was so taken with finding gown after gown for her that I didn't see the time speeding by, the sky darkening outside, the streetlights flooding the shop window. All that mattered was finding the perfect dress. I went to rail after rail trying to please her, desperate to find something that could out-do the red silk. Skin-tight satins, 50s circle frocks bustling with underskirts, beaded sari-inspired creations, fishtails, cathedral trains, nothing seemed to her taste. As dress after dress was tried and refused, I became almost frantic, tearing dresses from their hangers, rushing over to offer them to her, the floor of the shop strewn with taffeta, silks and satins as I pulled gown after gown from the rails, searching for the perfect one, willing it to be there somewhere.

And all this time, she stood there, on the shop pedestal, happily accepting gown after gown, holding them up against herself and … I hadn't noticed it till late on.

She barely looked at them.

Each one was held in front of her and gently shaken out as, deep in concentration, she stared steadily in front of herself, gazing at her own face in the mirror, before discarding it as useless.

It broke the spell. Was she sizing up my gowns, trying to

find one that was as beautiful as she was? But she hardly gave them a first glance, let alone a second. She just shook them out, stroking the fabrics down against her figure, sometimes scrunching the folds of a skirt and releasing it, always with that look on her face, staring deep into the mirror.

She turned to me, holding out the beaded bodice of one of our newest ranges with sad disappointment.

'Almost, but not quite,' she said, 'it's hard to describe what I'm looking for, really.'

I frowned and looked around the shop, at the sea of crystal white and ivory froth on the floor. Every dress had been tried and rejected. There were no more.

She bit her lip. 'Have you really nothing else?' she asked.

'A few in the stock room,' I said. 'Custom pieces, some older gowns from last season. We were getting ready for a sale, you see. I don't think there is anything there that would suit.'

I didn't want her to have last year's cast-offs. I wanted her to choose the red silk, or the sea-green dipped chiffon that had made her look like an elven princess.

'I'd be willing to try one, if you don't mind,' she said. 'I'll know it when we find it. I know I will.'

The minute I clicked on the light in the back room I regretted bringing her through. Out in the shop the dresses nestled on padded satin hangers, bathed in soft camellia-white light. Here the shadeless bulbs cast ugly shadows everywhere across the mess of the workspace. The dresses that had been put aside for the sale hung limply on wire hangers from a makeshift rail at the back of the room. With a wince of embarrassment I noticed that one had a torn sleeve hanging askew, the victim of a fight between two over-eager last minute brides who had both taken a fancy to it.

And there, in the middle of the stockroom, spread out across the square worktable, was The Jiltmaker. It was the shop's name for the ugliest frock we have ever had in stock. An eighties monstrosity of crushed silk, with a heavy skirt and frothed sleeves, in a shade of pink that resembled out-of-date taramasalata and starched lace that stuck out at crooked angles all round the neckline and hem. It had come to us in a job lot of dresses we had bought from a shop that was going out of business and we had instantly decided that if anything would make a groom run screaming from the altar then this dress would. So it became The Jiltmaker.

We had never tried to sell it. No bride in her right mind would have wanted it. We used it to scare uncooperative bridesmaids sometimes. The threat of what they 'might' have if they didn't behave made even the most self-absorbed girl a little more prepared to do as the bride wanted. Other than that it hung around the stockroom, gathering dust, and was occasionally borrowed for a Halloween or bad taste disco costume by one of the staff.

I didn't want her to see it. I'd already failed to find her anything that was sufficiently beautiful for her. I really didn't want her to think I would offer her this hideous thing. I tried to angle myself so that I blocked her view of the worktable.

'I'll bring some dresses through,' I said. 'You go back through to the shop.'

She smiled again and nodded.

'I'm sorry to be causing you all this trouble,' she said. Every word whisper soft and beautiful. Thank goodness she hadn't spotted The Jiltmaker.

'It's nothing,' I assured her, waving her through the door. I turned towards the back of the shop and pushed past the worktable, crushing the skirts of The Jiltmaker. The net underskirts rustled loudly against the silk.

'What's that?'

I almost swore. She hadn't left the room. She'd see the damned thing. I didn't want her to. I didn't want this hideous, ridiculous article to be the final story she had to tell about the shop. I could imagine her the next day with her friends, laughing with them over the paltry dresses she had been offered, 'And you'll never guess *what* they had hidden in their stock room!' as the crowning glory.

I pushed The Jiltmaker away from me, across the worktable. The silk whispered like kicked up autumn leaves.

'It's just something that we bought in a job lot sale,' I said. 'We won't be keeping it. It might be good for scraps.'

She edged round the side of the table, stepping over discarded shoeboxes and a pile of old editions of *Bride and Groom*.

'I know it's a sight, we didn't realise it was there,' I was saying, flustered and babbling. She ignored me, leaning over the dress, peering at it. For the first time since she'd entered the shop she was actually looking at something properly, taking in every discoloured plastic seed pearl, the dusty lace with its acrid plastic smell, the sickly silk. She stared at it. The look on her face said it all. You. Are. Ugly. Her nose wrinkled slightly. She reached out a hand towards the dress, lifted the skirts and, bending her head slightly closer, let it drop. The silk sighed gently as it fell back against the netting. She stood up.

'I want to try it on.'

It would have been funny if I hadn't felt like crying. She stood on the pedestal in the shop, the blancmange monstrosity hanging off her willowy frame. I had done my best with the lacing, but the workmanship on The Jiltmaker was so poor that not even she could wear it well. The skirts fell solidly to the floor, layer upon layer of netting so stiff that she didn't so much wear them as stand inside them. She stared resolutely at the mirror, taking herself in. Then she reached out both hands, grasped the skirt and swished it from one side to another.

She smiled.

She jumped off the pedestal. The silks rustled. I will say this for The Jiltmaker, foul as the dye job was, the silk that it was made from was of excellent quality. Moving it round the stock room, if you didn't look at it directly, was like walking through a woodland, listening to the wind playing gently in the trees.

She swirled round in the skirt and let out a cry of joy.

'How much is it?'

'Pardon?' There was no way that she was asking what I thought she might be asking.

'The dress. How much?'

'No, no it's not for sale.' There was no way I was letting her leave the shop wearing this fright.

She stopped swirling and looked disappointed.

'But it's the right one,' she said.

The customer is always right. Always. I tell myself that all the time. The girl who wanted her bridesmaids dressed as rabbits? Right. The girl who insisted on seven page boys, each in a different rainbow colour? Right. Even the girl who wanted a birdcage with live doves as a headdress. Right. Right. Right.

But not this. I couldn't let this one go.

'It's ... surely not.'

She looked back at the mirror. For a second I thought I saw sadness in her eyes, but she seemed to shake it away, drew herself up, looked down at the ugly frock and said in a clear, firm voice, 'I want to buy this dress.'

No. This just couldn't be right. I had wanted her to have the best. How could this beautiful woman choose such a mess to be her bridal gown? Did she want him to change his mind? Was The Jiltmaker about to live up to its name?

While she changed out of it, I tried to think of some way to talk her out of this. Perhaps I could tell her I'd lied. It was for sale but had been reserved? But did I really want to admit to selling such a foul thing?

'I know what you think,' she said, coming out of the dressing room with the thing draped over her arm and handing it to me to be boxed up. 'There's a reason. Truly there is. It's the best dress I could find for him.'

I frowned. 'Him?'

She smiled. 'Robert,' she said. 'Double-takes guaranteed, you said? Well this is the one. This is the one that will make him do a double-take. It's perfect.'

So that was it, she wanted something as a joke dress – something that would make everybody double-take because of how hideous it was. She wasn't the first bride to have that idea. They always regretted it. However funny it seemed at first, every bride wanted the same thing on their wedding day – to be the most beautiful creature on earth.

I draped the dress over the counter. It whispered, 'Shh shh shhhh.' I ignored it.

'I'm sure that's amusing to you at the moment, but really, I wouldn't …'

Behind us I heard the bell of the shopdoor. I hadn't locked up.

'Hello?'

I turned. In the doorway, his head turning from side to side as if looking round for something, stood a young man. A white cane in his hand tapped against a display case. The girl ran over to him, the bells on her skirt tinkling gently. He turned towards her and she kissed him on the cheek.

'Robert!'

'I was worried. You said you would be an hour at the most. I would have thought they would be closed by now,' he said.

She laughed. 'Well, it took longer than I thought. But I've found it. Oh, Robert it's perfect, it's beautiful.'

He smiled. 'Not as beautiful as you,' he said. 'You'll be the most beautiful bride in the world, and in the most wonderful dress I'm sure.'

For a second I saw her pause. But then she looked at him and beamed. 'You are going to *love* it,' she cried, with the excited joy that I had come to recognise as proof that a bride had truly found the dress she knew her groom would love. She wasn't pretending. I can tell. I've seen enough brides trying to convince themselves to love a dress they secretly know isn't the right one. This was real. She was genuinely looking forward to wearing that monstrosity.

She squeezed his arm. 'I need to pay,' she whispered and came back to the counter.

'You see,' she said, smiling at me. 'Those other dresses, they were, well they were lovely. But this one –' She motioned towards The Jiltmaker. 'This one *sounds* beautiful. I don't want someone else to tell him I'm coming down that aisle. I want him to hear me first. I want him to know I am close to him before I take his hand. I want to sound like a whisper in his ear, like the softest kiss being blown. I want what any bride wants – to be the most beautiful thing on earth.'

After they had gone, I stood in the shop for a while among the folds and waves of the discarded dresses, and wondered. The Jiltmaker lay on the counter, ready to be cleaned and boxed for her. I reached out for one of its skirts, closed my eyes tight and lifted it, letting the silk rustle and whisper.

It sounded like love.

# Two Right Hands

**Catriona Stewart**

I watch Siân and Beth bouncing on the trampoline, their long dark hair streaming in the wind. We should never have bought the wretched thing; they had as good a time with the box it came in. And we shouldn't have bought the new kitchen either. I've hardly had the chance to cook up a Hairy Bikers in there. Sian spots me through the window and waves like mad, then shouts at Beth who loses her balance trying to spot me. They don't know.

Gar could be enjoying his girls but he's still setting off every morning pretending to work and full of the wrath of God, like Taid. They shouldn't have lent us the money, he says. We didn't need a new kitchen, it was me and my big ideas. Mam agreed with Gar. She said, they never had what we've got; all the white goods, toys, foreign holidays. When she and Dad married, they saved and bought the house off the Council after we'd all finished school. I said it cost them pennies with the discount. Gar and I couldn't get a council house for love nor money. Even with me pulling my weight, working more than she ever did.

Gar and I argued all the time after that first letter from the bank, keeping our voices down so we didn't upset the girls. Fat lot of good it did in the end. He'd had a bit of work, cash in hand, at some farm, came back with a wad of notes. We could take the kids out for a treat, he said. Now who's talking, I said. I still don't understand why he went over the top after all that about me spending too much. He called me names I won't repeat, chucked the money at me and went upstairs, slamming doors. Next thing, he was hugging the girls and out the door. He didn't take his toothbrush so I thought he'd be back. Not a word for ten days now, and no money off him.

Mam's been brilliant. If Dad was still alive, he would've stopped her. Never a borrower or a lender be was his motto, no doubt another handy saying out of the Good Book. I've spent hours at the Council offices. I've told the girls their Dad's gone to find work. Same as what I told Mam and Mandy.

Sian remembers one of the names he called me, and tried it on me last night. Starts with the third letter in the alphabet. I told her straight out she can't repeat it. There's the phone now. They haven't cut us off yet.

'Mrs Hughes, is it? I'm afraid your husband, Gareth Hughes, has been taken to hospital. He's sustained an accident.'

Sustained an accident. They won't tell me any more than that. Mam's working in Aber today. I take the girls down the road to Mandy's shop. When I tell her that Gar's in hospital, she says she'll do the girls' hair. She'd lend me the car, she says, but I'm not insured, then she says, what the hell, locks up and takes me. The girls sit in the back and sing. I'm thinking he doesn't deserve their songs.

I'm dead calm, giving my details to reception and asking the

103

way to the ward. He's on his own behind curtains, hooked up to bleeping machines. His eyes are shut, and he's a terrible colour. Someone comes in behind me.

'Mrs Hughes? I'm Grace, the ward sister. He's sleeping at the moment. We've knocked him out.'

I sit there and try to take it in. Grace says Gar might lose part of his arm. The right one, for God's sake.

'We have to watch out for complications,' she tells me.

Complications. We've got those already. She's asking about Sian and Bethan, and then it sort of slips out, about the house being repossessed and the rest of it. Grace is a good name for her. We'll surely patch things up, there's a lot of it about, she says. I tell her it sounds like a disease and she says, well, maybe it is, a disease of modern society.

I go back to sit with Gar. I'm saying things I've not been able to say before. When you're in a bad mood with each other and you can see their face come over all angry, you get angry.

When I get back to Mandy's, she's kept the girls busy with little jobs, sorting the trays. Beth's showing me where they've washed the skirtings.

'You should let them help you more at home.'

What home? I give her a look over Sian's new hair, chocolate curls piled up on her head. Her eyes are made up too. She looks like Nefertiti. We'll probably be living in one room soon. Mandy's eyes say sorry for putting her foot in it.

'How is he?' she whispers when the girls fetch their coats.

'He might lose his right arm.'

'Gawd, Ceri. That's all you need.'

When the clock that's still on the wall creeps past five, I phone Mam and ask to go over. She's looking grim when we walk in. She gives the girls a hug and packs them off to the lounge sharpish.

'You look terrible, Ceri. Has he left you?'

'He did that already, ten days ago. He's in hospital, had an accident on that farm.'

Mam's a very calm person, had to survive thirty years with Dad. 'You'll have to come and live here now. There's no point waiting for the Council to help.'

I don't want to go back to Treflan, no way. Reminds me too much of my Dad, his Dad and dead Sundays.

'Mam, they're saying we're unintentionally homeless, high priority.'

'I don't know about that.'

'Don't know what?'

'Unintentional. You bought the house, put in a new kitchen, bought on credit.'

"Don't start that now.'

'Don't shout.'

'We were managing fine.'

Mam has this habit when she's upset. She winds her hair round her right ear and pulls it so her ear sticks out and pings back again. She has lovely hair, dark and thick. The girls are lucky, taking after her. I've got Dad's hair, another thing I can't forgive him for even if Gar says it's silky.

'Gareth worked in a car parts factory, Ceri. People buy cars when times are good.'

'Yeh, and we were told everything was going great in the country. Weren't we?'

Mam looks at me as if I'm an idiot. 'From where I'm sat, it's never looked that great.'

'So you've said. That's because you spend all day with old people needing their bums wiped.'

'I've told you before that it's not the old people who depress me, it's how we treat them.'

She starts to peel potatoes and gives me the carrots and a knife.

'You're moving out in two weeks, your husband's laid up. There'll be dozens after that council house in Tanygaer. You'll end up in the hostel.'

Mandy's Toyota pulls up as we finish dinner.

'I was thinking maybe you'd both want to go and see him, so I'll run you down and take the girls back home.'

Mam gives Mand a squeeze. 'You're a treasure. Yes, I'll go with her.' She lowers her voice but I hear. 'He walked out on them.'

'No thanks to you egging him on that everything was my fault. I'm going on my own.'

Sian's all ears and I'm frightened she'll chip in with the 'c' word, so I stop there. Mam fetches her jacket. She knows I won't row with her in front of the girls. On the ward, Gar looks like he's shrunk. Mam sits on the edge of the bed and puts her hand over his good one. She's always liked Gar, the son she never had. When she gets her hanky out, I start blubbing too. He wakes and says he's all dried up so she fetches a little sponge off the locker to wet his mouth. I want to tell her to get off the bed so I can hold his good hand. This is when the nurse comes in to check what's going on. He tells her that his arm's hurting a lot, so she goes off to get something. Mam moves at last and I nip round to hold his hand.

'She'll be back to give him an injection.'

'I know. And he's my husband.'

The nurse sticks a syringe in his good arm and Mam follows her out.

He's getting very sleepy. 'Am I?' he mumbles at me.

'What, love?'

'Your husband?'

'Course you are.'

Mam comes back to say she couldn't get much out of the nurse, and we should be getting home. In the cab, she starts again about moving in with her. The neighbours can move us. I say yes, to shut her up, thinking about the neighbours knowing our business.

'They'll know soon enough,' says the mind reader.

Mandy's got the girls to bed. She says there was a phone call, someone wanting to speak to me about Gareth's accident.

'Health and Safety Executive,' says Mam. 'There'll be an investigation.'

I sink down on the sofa and shut my eyes. 'No point speaking to me,' I say. 'I don't even know where he was working.'

'You're in this together,' says Mam. 'He wasn't going to booze it away.'

Mandy gives me a little wave from the door and disappears out into the night. There's nothing to hold Mam back now. 'A man has his pride. That's all I'm saying.'

'So have I.'

'It's different with a man.' I can't believe I'm hearing this. 'I'm not saying it's right, Ceri. Gareth's been raised to be the breadwinner. And, God help me, I'm not sure I did a good enough job with you. Your father was right. You're spoilt. Unintentionally homeless, my foot.'

I'm not listening to any more of this. I switch the light off while she's still talking. So I'm spoilt. Whose fault is that then?

In the morning, the girls are in bed with me, taking advantage.

Sian's a smart one. 'Will I be going to the same school, Mam?'

'Course you will. You heard Nain. We'll be living with her.'

'Good,' says Sian, sitting up and clapping her hands.

'And you won't be spending all your time watching telly.'

'We don't want to, do we, Sian?' asks Beth. 'We'll clean Nain's skirtings.'

'Don't be stupid,' Sian tells her.

Beth looks crushed so I tell her it's a lovely idea.

Mand drives me to the hospital again. She's going to take the girls to the beach and pick me up later. Gar's raised up a bit so he can see me coming.

'How's the arm?'

'Can't feel much.' He looks at his bandages. 'It's a blinking mess.'

'They want to speak to me about the accident. Was that the place you went before?'

'Yes. Should've had more sense than go back.'

'Beggars can't be choosers.'

The only time I've seen Gar cry is when he lost his job. It wasn't a great job but he liked his mates and he'd been there seven years.

'I could lose some of me right arm.'

'They said. Handy things, right arms, especially the hand.'

I'm squeezing his left hand really tight.

'It's not funny, Ceri.'

'Do you see me laughing?'

He shuts his eyes for a bit. He's thinking.

'I mean, imagine losing two right hands. Me and that one over there.'

He's nodding at me. I can see the ghost of a smile. He has lovely lips, my Gareth. It's just as well the doc arrives in the ward. I'm about to cause another complication. When I step out into the sun, the girls are hanging out of Mandy's car window, shouting at the seagulls. Mandy looks at me and gives me two thumbs up. I'm told I wear my heart on my sleeve.

# Painting Juliet

## Catherine Merriman

'What is it about plants?' Juliet asked, after the dozenth time I refused to paint her portrait.

I plucked a herbaceous attribute from the air. 'The stillness,' I said.

A good one. She didn't know whether to freeze, vegetable-like, or rant, her-like.

She wants me to paint her portrait. I'm not that kind of artist, I say. Not any more. I'm capable of it, of course, but I never paint girlfriends. Even frisky, amusing, twenty-eight-year-old girlfriends, who take inexplicable shines to middle-aged daubers. Call it tact, if you like. Or cowardice. I draw plants, not portraits. A portrait is a front(ish) view of a human being. Artists, despite our fleeting pretensions, are mere humans too, and human beings interact. Juliet and I have been interacting for several months. If I paint her portrait, I won't be painting an object, which just happens to be a person. I'll be painting a relationship.

Not a problem with plants. Interaction is not one of their strengths. Obligingly passive, undemanding things. Perfect sitters. They don't give a toss what they look like, leaves all askew, the odd petal droop – a matter of total indifference. They're happy to hold a pose for hours, or not hold it; they don't get miffed if you decide to take photos and work from them instead. You don't have to talk to them; though you can, of course, and their discretion is absolute. Nor do they object if you have a fag or a drink without offering them one, or fart or belch in their presence.

And, you know, there's a lot more demand for pictures of plants than of people. Oh yes. Take a look in your bookshelves. How many gardening books have you got? Plant identification books? Nature books? Use a lot of sketches, paintings, don't they? Now, how many books of human portraits have you got? None? Thought so. We all have a living to make.

I am sketching a nice docile yucca at the moment. Four feet high, with the appearance – and I know I'm hurting no one by saying this – of an upturned floor mop. *Yucca elephantipes*. So named, I assume, because the woody trunk suggests the emaciated leg of a midget elephant. She – all plants are female, obviously – is not a perfect specimen (two tatty fronds, as if a cat's taken passing exception to her) but I am drawing her as if she were. Now, could I do this with Juliet? No. Juliet is Juliet. It is precisely Juliet's unique peculiarities that make her Juliet. The yucca-ness of my friend here, on the other hand, is independent of such things. Her individual characteristics are irrelevant.

OK, I anticipate Juliet's objection. I'm not comparing like with like. The equivalent to 'yucca', as a generic, I suppose, should be 'human'. But try drawing a human, in the same detail I draw my yuccas. Does it end up simply 'human'? Does it hell. It ends up old, young, male, female, fat, slim, fair, dark. A unique, if sketchy, individual. There is no such thing, pictorially, as simply 'human'. Moreover, this individual, drawn with only cursory detail, wears an expression. Happy, sad, angry, contrite, bored, excited. Decisions, decisions. You wonder why I prefer drawing plants?

Juliet's women friends assume I must have painted or drawn her. He's an artist, is he? they say – giving me, if I'm present, a look half appraising (so *that's* an artist) half, well, *arch*, as if at any moment I might do something rampantly unconventional, possibly of a sexual nature. 'So,' they murmur, 'where are the pictures of you?'

'Nowhere,' Juliet replies, stiffly. The stiffness suggests that the admission, in a small way, humiliates her. Thus it is, undoubtedly, a criticism of me.

Would a plumber plumb the house of his girlfriend? A mechanic service her car? An architect design her house? Hell – I'm exampling myself into a corner; the answer's probably yes. Ah, but no. The trades are different, aren't they? How many ways are there of fixing a tap washer? Afterwards, the tap either drips or it doesn't. Same with an engine – it runs sweet or it doesn't. And the design of a house; well, no one would design a house for a girlfriend without consulting her, finding out what she wants. It would be a shared project; his execution moulded by her needs and desires.

While a portrait. It would be *for* her, but with no input *from* her, except as subject matter. Portraits express the artist's view of the subject, not the subject's view of themselves. And here, we're getting to the crunch. She wants my view of her. I don't want to give it to her.

Well, got there in the end. Forget all the tosh. We're good at making everything their fault, aren't we? The fact is that if I paint her portrait – a proper portrait, not a camera-snap equivalent – I will be revealing myself to her – myself, vis-a-vis her – and this I balk at.

I have told her. An attempt at honesty. The reason I won't paint your portrait, I say, is because if I do it properly, I would be exposing myself to you (don't snigger) with no reciprocation. And, I add (on thinner ice now, but mere exposure doesn't seem enough), what I revealed would, in all probability, be scoffed at by you. I'd be making myself vulnerable. The old boy-girl thing. Loin-girding approach by boy, castrating rejection by girl.

'For God's sake,' she says, rolling her eyes. 'Don't be ridiculous.'

'No,' I say firmly. 'It's you who's ridiculous. There is no guarantee you'd like it. It might even offend you.'

This is a mistake. The thin ice shatters. 'Since when,' she hisses, 'did offending me worry you? And when have I ever, *ever* scorned your work?' She exits violently, frightening the door. It shakes for several seconds. But she returns later, much calmer. 'What I'd really appreciate,' she says, in a quiet, reasonable voice, 'is the mere fact that you'd painted my portrait. That's more important to me than what the picture looks like.'

'Good heavens,' I say. 'Really? So you wouldn't need to see

it? I could just slap the paint around, prove I've done it, and then hide it away somewhere?'

She smiles tolerantly. What a joker. Explains that of course she'd want to see it. She's just promising that she'll be nice about it. Take into account its existence, the work that went into it, as well as its actual appearance.

Terrific. So now she's saying that she will want to see the picture, and will absorb any information it conveys (because how can she not?) but will keep her response to this, tactfully, to herself. What an offer. Not only will she be privy to my true, artistically expressed feelings about her, but her reaction to these feelings will remain under wraps. How can I refuse?

'Anyway,' she cajoles, 'what will be so revealing about the portrait? What have you got to hide?'

This is a very intelligent question. Juliet – contrary to any impression I might have given – is very intelligent. Another way in which she differs from plants. The answer, of course, is that I don't know – I can't know – until I paint the portrait. Like any act of creation, it is a process with an unknown end. Not totally unknown – it will, at least in my own mind, centre on Juliet, or some vital aspect of her – or, indeed, us – but how, exactly, remains to be seen. After all, if you knew what the end-product of a creative work was going to be, why bother with the toil of getting there?

This interests her. (I have foolishly argued my case aloud.) A voyage of discovery. 'Yeah,' I say. 'Me voyaging, you discovering.'

'You discovering too,' she cries, 'and so what?' She is pink with frustration. (Quite an interesting pink, traces of carmine.) 'It is not a contest,' she says. 'Who can hide most from whom. We're meant to be in love.'

This is true. We are. Meant to be. OK, I say. I have a problem. I admit it freely. Us problematic males do. You females can lay your hopes and fears and needs and desires on the slab for anyone to pick over, but we blokes value our privacy. We are mysterious creatures, even to ourselves, and that's how we like it.

'Aha!' she cries. 'Aha! So it's not *my* reaction to a portrait that's stopping you, it's *yours*.'

For a moment I am dumbfounded. 'I didn't say that,' I mutter.

'Yes, you did,' she retorts.

See, you don't get this with yuccas. They don't tire your brain. Answer back. Provoke you into saying things that may or may not be true.

OK, I say finally, because I refuse to be drawn into further argument. God knows where it will end. Capitulate now. You win. I'll do it. She claps her hands. I have delighted her, and that's a nice feeling. Extraordinarily nice. I hadn't anticipated that. But there are rules, I say sternly. She nods. Anything, anything. Anything, eh? Wickedness tempts, but a carte blanche forces responsibility. Why am I so mature, dammit? So here they are: all reasonable rules. First: no looking till it's finished. Nod nod nod. She expected that. Understands I can't work with eyes over my shoulder. Especially not hers. Second: no enquiries over progress. No 'how's it going?' even. Nod nod

nod. Oh, those bright, forget-me-not eyes. Third and last: no demands for an explanation when it's over. The picture must be enough. I'm a visual artist. If I wanted to explain myself verbally, I'd be something else.

We are agreed. We have set aside time. I'm nervous, but it's a stewing nervousness, not unpleasant. It promises a result. First, the sketches. This is the part I particularly don't want her to see, or comment on, because it can stop me dead. I'm good at sketching. It's what I do, if I'm honest, when I draw my plants. It's all they want. A clear, painted-in sketch. She'd like these sketches of mine. If I painted one in, that would probably be enough. For her, that is. But if I'm going to do this at all, let's do it properly. Let's do it for me. Sketches are just the starting point.

It's the hand moving that stimulates the brain. When the hand is free, experimental, unrestrained. No way of knowing which way to go until I've roughed it out, seen it. Recognised it. Takes a lot of sketches, but she's being patient. And, I have to admit, she's a lovely subject to draw. My hand feels comfortable. Doesn't dither. Seems to know intuitively where to go.

Right. I've decided on a whole body portrait. I've tried heads, and head and shoulders, but they all look decapitated. Partial. I need the whole of her. And I don't want background detail. Nothing that suggests a setting. Juliet does not belong anywhere. She is just Juliet. So. Standing? Sitting? Lying? Naked? Clothed?

She has a green dress I keep getting flashes of. A soft sheath dress, clingy T-shirt material. I've asked her to put it on, and it looks kind of right. But only kind of. Nakedness appeals too, though not for the obvious reasons. Not even because it suggests intimacy. And not even because I can see she likes the idea. Wanton woman – the point of this is to satisfy me, not indulge her. But she does look good naked. Confident, natural.

I'll start with nakedness; see how it runs. I can always overpaint. I need her standing, legs together. Weight on one hip if she wants to. As long as she's upright, and doesn't give me daylight between her thighs. She's tall and slim. Lying or sitting you wouldn't see it, and tall and slim is her. Her for me, that is.

Well, I've got a general painty outline, and even the brush strokes to go with it, but her middle section is proving a problem. Her breasts, particularly. Not sure why, but they are. Bloody things. Too substantial. Too fleshy. Too animal. I need lightness, less solidity.

But I'm going to enjoy the hair. Wild red hair. Pile on the henna, I've told her.

Shit. Something isn't working. Stand back. It's not right. Juliet can see my face.

'Problems?' she says, deeply sympathetic. She's been a dream since I started doing this; no criticism, nothing's too much trouble. A revelation.

'Shut up,' I reply. 'I'm thinking.'

She's not offended. Not remotely. She's flattered. All this wrestling concentration, over her. Except it isn't, of course. It's over me.

It's no good. Start again. I repaint the canvas. Green. The

entire thing. A plain green canvas. And for a terrible few hours that's where I want to leave it. As if the colour says it all. She would be appalled, but that's not my consideration. I am appalled at myself. It shows a lack of complexity. A mental laziness, even.

Face it, I am a lazy bugger. It's years since I've done this. Years of sketching plants, painting them in, no effort at all. Story of my life. Yes, the story of my life.

Dim, too. I say it to myself, hear it in my ears, and still take hours to grasp it. The green is right. But as background. This is where she comes from.

Yes! Got it. Got it. Christ, I even understand it. No, wait, it rings bells. It's been done before. Hell. But does that matter? Think, think. No. It's OK. The reference works. The image is right. If I can capture it.

Juliet is delighted with my attitude. My commitment. This is a side of me, she says, she has been longing to see. A true artist. When not fighting with the painting I am distracted and monosyllabic; I can't think what she finds attractive about this, but there's no accounting for female taste. I am slightly proud of myself, though. I do feel committed. And, dammit, I am enjoying myself. Who'd have thought it?

I've put as much green as I can get away with into her skin tone. She's got to be distinct from the background, but connected to it. As if she has *emerged* from it. I think it works. I've solved the breast problem. I was getting hung up on what they actually looked like, rather than what I felt about them, and her. A change of perspective, that's all it took. Now there they are: as fragile, blow-in-the-breeze as the rest of her. Not that I see women's flesh as fragile, you understand – anything but – but fragile it has to be. Fragility suggests all the right things: preciousness, perfection, the sense of something caught between too-soon (sturdily immature) and too-late (wilted, overblown). It means extraordinary, undeserved luck.

Good God. Listen to me. Sentimental fool.

Now I'm buzzing. This is right right right. All those years of practice, and I'm within tendrils of the end. I am reassured, pathetically, by the fact that Juliet will never know my journey here. Silly me; of course I'm safe. She thinks I've been at the point I've just discovered for months, and she'll never know otherwise.

She was absolutely right, too, about the act of painting being more important than the final appearance, though not in the way she meant. She was thinking of herself, not me.

There we are. Complete. Perfect. The image, necessarily, is more abstract than Juliet might have wished, but it's right, and that's what matters. She'll recognise herself. I haven't played around with her face; it's unmistakably her. Doing that didn't even feel like a concession. In fact it felt essential. Ambiguity about her identity would be a cop-out.

Stand back from it. Look at those hands. An *Amaranthus* would be jealous. And the burnished hair – eat your heart out, *Acer palmatum purpureum*. Glad I chose lily rather than orchid between her legs. Orchid's more genital but too obvious, and lily's more approachable, and just as sexy. My Woman of Flowers. The original, if you remember your folk tales, was a lady specially created to partner some poor sod cursed never to have a mortal wife. She was unfaithful to him and in the end conspired to kill him. Well, yes. Women aren't floral Lego. Take one on, and they can hurt you.

Wonder if Juliet knows the story? Maybe, maybe not. I'll show it to her now. But no explanations. I warned her.

# The Guilty Party

## Jo Mazelis

Because of love there was beauty even in the endless rain. Even in the fast growing weeds in the garden. Even in the fact that they had reached now an age when they each needed spectacles; especially on a day such as this when clouds hang grey and low diminishing the anaemic sun.

But still, it was beautiful because there was much to be grateful for; the house was dry and the roof didn't leak, and it was warm enough, especially if they stayed in bed, reading books and taking it in turns to run to the cold kitchen to make tea.

He is reading a book about Laurel Canyon, California in the 1960s; she, a collection of modern poetry.

*Joni Mitchell is popping in for tea and smokes with David Crosby, and James Taylor lives across the street and then maybe Bob Dylan happens to drop in as he's visiting from some place else. And it's kind of like heaven with orange Pekoe tea and songs just casually zinging off the walls and ceiling, and blue, blue sky and it never rains there.*

And it's Sunday and it's May and the man is not her husband. And she is not his wife.

So much for beauty.

Cathy and Martin had been lovers for so long they had almost forgotten it was a secret. That at first there had been so much lust and guilt. Then they had been wild and hungry. Seventeen years ago. Her thighs aching and bruised. Him hard before she'd even touched him.

She turns the page. Does not wet her finger with her tongue in order to do so. As his wife does. She sighs to find a familiar poem. It is called 'Penitence'. She had forgotten its title. But not the deer struck by a car and how the man in the poem somehow becomes the deer. She is about to suggest she read it aloud, then thinks better of it. Their shared silence is like the warm water in an Italian Lake. Lago di Garda where they had a mid-week break last summer.

The doorbell rings.

Sometimes it rings all on its own; it's one of those cordless radio jobs. A signal passes from the button outside the door to the bell in the hall, but something, perhaps someone pressing the button of their car key, can also set the doorbell off.

'Who's that?' she says.

It's early, it's Sunday, they are still in bed, reading and drinking tea.

He shrugs even though her question was entirely rhetorical.

Her cat is capable of rattling the low letterbox when it wants to come in, but the doorbell is too high up.

Besides it's raining and so the black and white cat is lying on the foot of the bed though it really wanted to lie on the man's neck and had to be pushed away five times before it gave up. Cats see humans as useful pieces of furniture at certain times, and servants at others. He sees cats as pointless.

Cathy takes off her glasses, then gets out of bed, carefully folding back her half of the duvet to keep the warm bit warm. She puts on a thin silky dressing gown which she bought from T K Maxx. She has a warmer dressing gown in a drawer, it's pink and fluffy, but not at all sexy, and she's still not ready to betray herself or betray him or betray this thing they have going for themselves.

This is why we have affairs. Not just for the sex, she gets enough of that from her husband when he's around and it's good, it's fine, it's dandy. But it does not make her feel powerful. Her fault, she supposes, the first time she let a little thing like feeling cold propel her into wrapping herself up in the lumpy pink gown.

The doorbell rings again.

She hurries from the room and towards the stairs, and it is cold, she can feel an icy draft pinpricking over her skin. There is no spy hole in her front door which is something she's always meant to get around to doing but hasn't yet. If it was night, still dark out, if she were alone in the house, she'd call out, 'Who's there?' before opening the door and then if no reply came, she'd be terrified, imagining all sorts all night long, exhausted by morning, worn out by her raging mind. Another reason to take a lover.

Now the wind gusts and the rain has turned to sleet, it pings tinnily as if thrown in handfuls on the big stained glass window at the turn on the stairs. Her flesh is all goosebumps, her nipples are erect – she will have to keep one arm crossed in front of her to hide them.

She opens the door and the freezing wind and rain seem to seize this opportunity to punish her, to whip at her silky dressing gown, get a good look at those bare legs of hers, get some kind of wet t-shirt effect going on too.

There's a woman on the doorstep, she's wet and wind-whipped even though she's holding an umbrella.

'Can I come in,' she says, and without waiting for an answer, she is coming forward as though pushed by the implacable wind. She slams the door behind her and shuts her ragged black umbrella. Cathy notices how it is dripping rapidly from its spike and making a puddle on her new wooden floor. And the woman is dripping too. She's dripping from the hem of her stone-coloured mackintosh, dripping from her hair and pink gleaming fingers, dripping from her eyelashes and from the tip of her reddened nose. She shakes her head slightly like a feeble dog and a few fine droplets fly off. Cathy feels one or two splash her face.

The woman smiles quickly. A perfunctory smile more like a facial tic really.

'Listen …' Cathy begins to say, but the woman interrupts her. What Cathy was going to say was, Listen, I know it's terrible out there, but whatever you're selling, whether it's God or double glazing or cheaper electricity, I'm not buying, so if you don't mind …

124

But the woman is too quick, she spits out the very same word, but louder and with more emphasis and animation. 'Listen!' she says and chops violently at the air with the hand which is not holding the umbrella.

There is a moment when neither speaks; both have staked a claim on this silence. Then the woman leans the umbrella against the cold radiator and tilts her head to one side as if listening. Cathy, struck dumb by incomprehension, also strains to hear, imagining some terror in the street outside that has chased this woman here. Suddenly the woman's expression changes, now her eyes are shining and wild with triumph, she leans forward, whispers, 'He is here!'

Upstairs the bed creaks; Martin is shifting position in the bed, leaning over to put his mug of tea on the bedside table.

Cathy opens her mouth, breathes in quickly in preparation for speech, but the woman pre-empts her again.

'Listen!' The woman's face is contorted with an expression of lunatic urgency. 'I know all about you,' she says and it's horribly affecting; the impact of these words silences Cathy.

'Oh yes, I know all about you. Look at you! Look at yourself! Will you look at yourself? *Can* you look at yourself? You slut. You whore. You scum of the earth!'

At this moment the tirade of abuse is halted, because the paper boy is heaving, forcing, ramming, jam-packing the big fat damp supplement-heavy *Sunday Times* through the letterbox and he manages to poke the strange woman in the back of her leg, startling her.

The woman does a weird little hop, turns and sneers at the

newspaper where it has been disgorged, limp, wet, torn and pulpy in places, then she turns to Cathy again.

'You thought no one would know, didn't you? You thought you could get away with it, didn't you? Well, let me tell you, there is always someone watching. Always!' She did not raise her voice as she spoke, but used a strange croaky whisper that was even worse, like something from a horror movie.

'I …' Cathy says. She had meant to be forceful, but the single syllable sounds more like a yelp of pain.

The noise of it seems like a signal to action for the woman in the stone-coloured raincoat. The absurd lady spy mackintosh, the black umbrella with its broken spokes, its curved handle, its dangerous spike. A small puddle of water is gathering at her feet; drop a small electrical appliance into it (still plugged in and switched on obviously) and watch her melt as the sparks fly!

This idea swept briefly through Cathy's mind at the exact same minute that a magpie flew past the bedroom window *just* catching at Martin's eye. Seeing it like that, a brief blur of black and white, he had the distinct impression that it was Cathy's cat soaring through the air.

As she thought about electrocuting the woman, possibly a nervous smirk twitched and curled at the edge of her lip. Or perhaps it was that she had dared to make a noise. Or maybe the woman had read Cathy's mind. Whatever it was, she leapt forward suddenly and landed a resounding slap across Cathy's cheek. It was hard enough to force Cathy's head to turn.

The shock of it!

No one had ever struck Cathy before. No one.

But she did not cry out. Too surprised really. And afraid.

Afraid to call Martin down to rescue her, because, of course, *this was his wife*.

The woman was breathing noisily through her nose; her mouth was a tight, fleshless, defiant line, her nostrils flared.

Cathy's mouth must have dropped open in surprise. Had she been waiting for this all along? Her punishment. Her first instinct was to bring her hand up to her cheek to measure its heat, the damage done, to nurse and protect it, but she was too slow, the woman hit her again. Oh god, in the same place, but this time catching her ear somehow too.

The two women stared at one another. Cathy said, 'I'm sorry, can't we be reasonable about ...'

And for a third time the woman slapped her, and Hell! She was improving her technique with practice, making her hand land with more force, more noise and bone-juddering weight.

And this time she added an extra backhanded slap for Cathy's other cheek on her return swing.

'Slut!' she hissed, then she turned and opened the front door. Cold damp air gusted in, and the woman slipped away quicker than a magician's assistant stepping into a magic cabinet, the damp flaps of her pale mackintosh whipping out of sight and barely escaped being snatched by the briskly shut door.

Cathy just stood there for a moment, mouth open, gasping for air. She checked that the door was indeed closed, then she went up the stairs and into the bedroom.

Martin didn't look up, or at least not until she'd stood there by the bed breathing dramatically for some seconds.

'Cathy? Cathy, what's up? Who was there? God, your face!'

At last she manages to speak. 'She hit me, oh God, she hit me!' She lifted trembling fingers to her burning cheeks, her red buzzing ear.

'What?'

'Your wife.'

'What?'

'Your bloody wife. She knows … Oh, Jesus Christ.'

'My wife's in Australia.'

'She's not, she was here in a bloody stupid wet raincoat and she hit me!'

He gets out of bed, puts his arms around her, urges her to sit on the edge of the bed, studies her face.

'You need to put some ice on this,' he says. 'Who the hell did it?'

'Your wife! Your bloody sodding lunatic wife!'

'Helen? But she's in Australia for the conference, there's pictures on Facebook of her in front of Ayers Rock, holding a bloody koala, I saw her onto the plane myself!'

'It was her. She called me a whore. She said she knew.' Cathy realizes that some of her teeth feel odd, as if they've been loosened, and begins at last to cry. 'Then who the hell was it? Who?'

'I don't know. How would I know? Some nutter maybe? Got the wrong house? I told you your 59 looks like a 50 – tail's not long enough on the nine. What did she look like?'

128

He stops talking while she sobs.

'I'll get ice.'

He comes back with a packet of frozen petit pois and another of spinach, holds her face sandwiched between them, watches her with concern. Her tears begin at last to subside.

'I didn't hear a thing,' he said. 'Why didn't you call out?'

'Because I thought it was your wife!' Cathy said through clenched teeth, then with a wail added, 'so I just stood there and let her hit me!'

*

The following week they met for coffee in Café Nero. They found a table by the window which looked out at the castle across the road. He sat with his back to the view. She was facing him. She sprinkled brown sugar on the frothy surface of her cappuccino, ate it with a spoon. She'd put concealer over her bruises, but they still showed blue and yellowish on her cheekbones and beneath one eye.

He glances around the café feeling uncomfortable, afraid that someone will notice her face and think that he's a wife beater. He is glad she has her back to the other customers. She looks awful.

She is staring past him, her eyes narrowing, a frown making a black line above her nose.

Slowly, as if lifted to a hypnotist's command, she raises one hand, the index finger pointing.

'It's her.'

He swivels his head to see.

'Where?'

'There.'

'Where?'

'Handing out leaflets. Next to the man with the sign.'

Finally he sees her, this woman who his lover mistook for his wife. A scrawny crow of a woman in a pale raincoat. Legs with no shape to them. Scuffed shoes. Shouting in the street. Pointing at the sign when someone refuses a leaflet.

*The Wages of Sin is Death.*

Shouting, 'Listen, sinners!'

How could anyone think that he would marry her? Or stay married to a woman like that?

'It's over,' he said.

She could feel the hand striking her cheek again, the terrifying force of it, her powerlessness.

'Yes,' she said. 'Over.'

# The Foolish Maid

**Dilys Cadwaladr**

*translated by Cathryn Charnell-White*

The former teacher of Llanedwyn Girls' School gazed at the tip of her shoe, and a smile spread across her pale face – a cold, dignified face that did not smile too often. The shoe delighted her! With a ringed right hand, she pulled the collar of her beaver coat closer around her neck and pretended to sleep in her chair in the shade of the eaves of 'Bel Vista'.

The most visible marks on her cheeks were those made by narrow responsibilities, and there was a little self-righteousness in the cut of her jaw. If her lips were once tender and full, they were now pressed tight by the worries of her profession; and nothing remained but some vestige of tender yearning. But that vestige remained unchanged, even after forty years of intent self-discipline.

There were no traces of life's storms on her forehead, nor around her eyes. Yet the signs of many a dry summer could be seen there. She looked gentler when her eyes were closed, as their superficial gleam could not be seen – it was a coldness that had once been fire. Her body was in good condition. The neck under her collar was smooth like an alabaster column, and the bosom under the folds of the velvet dress was full; but there was no fullness of promise in her breasts! She wore a diamond ring on the third finger of her left hand, but no one asked the name of the man who had pledged himself to her. She also knew that this ring would never be replaced by a plain gold band.

A fortnight of the holiday had passed. This was the longest holiday of her life. There was 'no going back' after the five weeks. The last term had witnessed the end of forty years of labour and the beginning of that period without a horizon called the 'twilight' of life. But the afternoon of Miss Pugh's life had barely passed. The sunlight still lingered on the occasional high path; and the boundaries were not clearly defined so far. And it was right to say that Miss Pugh did not look to the west too often.

For that matter, when she opened her eyes, she looked towards the north, towards Llanedwyn, towards the mountains; and the thrill of the labour of many years swept over her until it caused her to sink further into the depths of her easy chair and take a deeper breath.

The hardest thing for her now was not to bother; her mind insisted on worrying constantly about trivial details. When the hotel bell rang, from time to time, Miss Pugh jumped straight out of her chair, and her heart raced under the pressure of some silent need. As she rested on the veranda, she tried to assert her right to stretch out and to turn a deaf ear when the bell rang; a right to walk leisurely along the paths of Llandrindod, and idle all day long if she insisted. But routine is a strange thing.

She had been oppressed for half her life by an alert conscience; and she completely failed to drink the unfamiliar wine of idleness.

She had a store of forty years of frugality to her name in the bank, and a comfortable annuity apportioned for her in the Education Office. She knew that she would now have a month's holiday every year at the Bel Vista hotel to change air and change environment, not to mention the hope of seeing new faces. The spinster would not confess to herself for a moment that there was another hope, secret and intense, in her breast; a hope that was resurrected without fail every summer, despite being pushed to the depths of her soul every winter – a hope of seeing 'The Face' once again.

In her mind, The Face had not changed through the years. The fervent light in his eyes was the same; the impatient pride in his lips was the same, the playful smile, and the sudden sadness, that would fall alternately on his fair cheeks like an April shower.

It was a romantic, wild face that encapsulated many foolish dreams; a little fun too: eyes that did not look too far into the future; lips that sucked the honey of the moment without worrying what fruit it would taste tomorrow.

But on the chair on the veranda, Mary Pugh remembered that those lips had once implored her too, that those eyes had begged her to throw caution to the wind and take the blessings of the gods when they extended their arms.

She also remembered, as her hand caressed the smooth fur of her new coat, that she had wept at night, heartbroken because she did not know what to do for the best – walk the quiet valley between the hedges of respectability, or climb the exposed slopes and brave tomorrow's storm to have today love's sunlight on the uncertain path.

She remembered the sleepless hours one night when she had been closest to sneering at safety, simply because the memory of a kiss was still on her lips.

She remembered the frivolity that came to those eyes the following night when she chose the daily bread and the warmth of the sheltered roads instead of the blessed feasts of the fickle gods.

When, in turn, the summer came, after forsaking love, a rebellion arose. She felt the urge to climb the wild paths again; but the monthly salary placed a fetter around her feet; and the desire weakened from year to year, leaving her by now, at the end of her work, almost content.

But today, like a contradiction to the constant labour, behold, the memory of it trespassed on her leisure. But the hedges had grown by now; and despite removing the fetter, it was too difficult to cut through them. And by now, what was the point of climbing, while she was on her own? Love does not want silver hair; and there is no venturing at night. It did not occur to her that The Face might also have changed and that the fervent light had become dull, that the frivolity had turned into stubborn disbelief …

The voices of other guests broke her reverie. She turned her head to watch them climbing the garden path towards the house. Every face was unfamiliar to her; but there was one who followed the others – somewhat slower due to a shortness of breath.

Miss Pugh heard the young ones mocking the middle-aged man as they passed, and laughing benevolently at his fatigue. He stopped to rest awhile by the veranda, and she saw his eyes for the first time. Some of the pride remained in them!

The tip-tap of Miss Pugh's shoe on the veranda stopped, and she rested her ringed hand in astonishment on her thigh.

After catching his breath, the man looked at her rather apologetically; and he said in a hesitant voice, with a wintry smile, 'The young must have the chance to laugh a little, madam; and we must tolerate frivolity every now and then.' Then he half-questioned more seriously, 'Excuse me, did you hear the dinner bell?'

But Miss Pugh did not have a chance to reply. The bell rang as he spoke, and old habit caused the teacher to jump to her feet.

# Endings

## Jo Verity

Shutting the front door, he waits, watching the figure of the doctor wavering and dissolving beyond the frosted glass. He passes down the silent hall, through the kitchen to the back door where he stands on the step, sucking in the damp afternoon. The wind stirs the sycamore tree at the end of the garden, releasing a shower of leaves to join the others on the threadbare grass.

He fills the kettle up to the brown tide-mark, pauses, and then pours half the water away before flicking the switch. While it boils, he rearranges the pots of chrysanthemums that stand on the low wall at the edge of the lawn, pulling and turning them, clay rasping on brick.

A young-ish woman emerges from the adjoining house and goes through the motions of checking the washing hanging on the rotary clothes-line. She approaches the fence dividing the gardens, feigning surprise. 'Hi, Alex. Didn't notice you there.' She wrinkles her nose and glances back at the limp towels. 'Wetter than when I pegged them out.' Her pencilled eyebrows dip in a frown. 'How's Ruthie?'

He stares at her tanned face and coarse blonde hair. 'Much the same, thanks, Linda.'

'Only I thought I saw the doctor leaving just now.' Linda has strong white teeth. Her full lips are iridescent with lipstick, plum-coloured like a ripe bruise.

'Yes. He calls most days.' Turning his head towards the door he says, 'I'd better get back. Kettle's boiling.'

'Give her my love, won't you?' She looks away, towards the tree. 'Sorry I haven't been in for a while. We've been ever so busy at work. And I've had a bit of a cold.' She gives a confirmatory cough.

'No worries. I'll tell Ruth,' he emphasises the correct form of his wife's name, 'that you were asking.'

He drops a tea bag into a blue-and-white-ringed mug, raises the kettle then places it back on the stand and, instead, fills a glass with tap water. The worktop is barely visible between the clutter of unwashed crockery. He walks around the kitchen, sipping the water, circling the kitchen table upon which a glazed fruit bowl, heaped with blackening bananas and dull-skinned oranges, sits surrounded by junk mail. He tips the un-drunk water down the sink and nudges the empty glass between the dirty plates and mugs.

The stairs creak beneath his listless tread. At the top he glances down, noticing the pack of toilet rolls and carton of toothpaste which he has already passed a dozen times. 'Damn.' But he doesn't go back for them.

The bedroom door is ajar. He leans his head towards the opening and calls gently, 'It's only me. Are you awake?'

She is lying on 'her' side of the bed. He has been sleeping in the spare room since she came home from the hospital, but she keeps to the side which she chose the very first night they slept together. 'Hi, Only You.' Turning her head towards his voice, she smiles but does not open her eyes then she lifts her right arm from beneath the sheet and pats the empty place beside her.

He stacks pillows to form a backrest against the headboard and sits down, swinging his legs up on to the bed. Perched here, higher than and slightly behind her, he can see what remains of her hair – her beautiful red hair – dotted in scrappy clumps across her scalp. There are hairs on the pillowcase and on the sheet. He screws his eyes tight shut and breathes deeply. 'Anything you want, love?'

'I'm fine, thanks.' She feels for his hand and he takes hers with its square nails and smattering of freckles. She runs her tongue across her flaky lips. 'What've you been doing?'

'Pottering. Gardening. Oh, Linda sends her love. Says she'll be in to see you when …'

'That's kind.' She closes her eyes again.

How big her nose looks; how prominent the pores around her nostrils; how sallow her skin.

'Are they managing without you at the office?' she murmurs.

'Sure. Everything's fine. Don't worry. I'd better get on …' But she's asleep again. He lays her hand back on the cover and eases himself off the bed.


Rinsing a bowl under the tap, he dries it and fills it to the brim with cornflakes. He sniffs the carton of milk before pouring it over the cereal then sprinkles the whole lot with granulated sugar from the bag.

It is not yet four o'clock but, in the living room, the heavy velvet curtains are shut, excluding the thin October sunlight. The muted television flickers in the corner; a vase of flowers, petals dropping, water murky, sits on the mantelpiece; badly-folded newspapers spill off the coffee table. The air smells of freesias and burnt toast.

He slumps on the sofa and begins eating the cornflakes, pausing to rummage for the remote control beneath the cushions then, dipping it towards the set, he flicks through the silent channels. Cartoons. Advertisements. Cooking. More cartoons. He flicks again and again and again, the garish images, frantic and meaningless, reach his eyes but make it no further.

Another flick and it's a news channel. He pauses. A newsreader, matt-browed, slick-haired, is mouthing words, his face solemn with the gravity of whatever he's saying. The picture switches to a windswept moor. Men in fluorescent yellow tabards, with ropes and climbing gear, are manoeuvring around some kind of opening in the ground.

Holding the bowl to his chin and, ignoring the droplets of milk that drip on to his shirt, he scoops cereal into his mouth.

Next, a series of still photographs. A black and white dog. Small, with a wiry coat and legs too thin for its body. A couple on a winter beach, the dog tucked beneath the woman's arm, the man pointing at something out to sea. Now, back on the moor, the same woman, clearly agitated, speaks soundlessly into the reporter's microphone and points over her shoulder, towards the opening.

A knock at the front door interrupts the silence and, setting the empty bowl down on the carpet, he goes to open it, walking slowly, as though he has all the time in the world. A nurse stands in the tiled porch, brisk and neat, and without waiting to be invited in, she squeezes past him, a whiff of cigarette smoke coming off the navy fleece she wears over her white uniform. 'How is she?'

He shrugs. 'The same.'

'And how about you?' She touches his arm. 'Look, I'm going to be here for at least an hour. Why don't you get a breath of air? A change of scene.' Her plain face is a mask of optimism and he can offer no reason why he shouldn't.

It is getting on for five o'clock and the light has gone. The wind swirls dry leaves across the pavement, herding them against the garden wall. He will walk for half an hour, then turn back. That should satisfy her. By the time he reaches the end of the street, he wishes that he'd put on a thicker jacket. He steps up the pace, picturing his heart pumping faster and faster, pushing blood through arteries and veins, warming him, keeping him alive, and he lays a hand over the spot where he imagines his heart to be.

The streets are busy. Commuters returning home from work. Parents collecting and delivering children to football practice or music lessons. Lights coming on in kitchens and living rooms. Cooking smells. People waiting at bus stops.

He walks urgently but aimlessly and after twenty minutes he arrives at a small shopping centre. He thinks it odd that

140

they never shop here, then remembers that Ruth prefers the supermarket on the other side of town because it stocks a wide range of organic vegetables.

Determined to prove to the nurse that he has, indeed, 'had a change of scene', he decides to take something back for Ruth. He studies the parade of shops. Hairdresser. Travel agent. Dry cleaners. Everything they offer serves to emphasise her predicament.

There's a pharmacy, but he has spent too many dreary hours hanging about, waiting for prescriptions or searching through catalogues of terrifying invalid aids.

A flower stall. Please, no more flowers. No more roses or lilies or gerberas or irises. He can't stand the smug things, perfect and unnatural, delivered to the door by strangers, facile messages taped to their fancy cellophane wrappers.

The sugary smell of childhood seeps out of the newsagents, luring him in. He glances around, hoping to spot something that will do. Magazines, bursting with bright-eyed women. Party hats and bubble mixture. A dozen or more varieties of crisps. Greetings cards. Calendars, the coming year set out in neat rows. Sweets and chocolate. *Chocolate.* He grabs a small bar of bitter chocolate and joins the queue, suddenly eager to be home. As he stands, fumbling through his pockets, he realises that he has come out without any money. 'Shit.' He slips the chocolate bar on to the nearest shelf and hurries out.

Breaking into a jog, he exchanges the neon-lit shop windows for the shadows of suburban streets. Without meaning to, he avoids the cracks between the paving stones and, once set on this tack, the fear of hitting one becomes so intense that he takes to the road.

He has forgotten his keys, too, and has to knock. The light comes on in the hall and the nurse opens the door. She inspects his face, theatrically. 'That's better. Not quite so pasty.' She takes her jacket from the newel post. 'I'll be off then. She's nice and comfy. I've given her a fresh nightie and changed her pad.'

'Thanks, Margaret.' He nods and holds the door open, staring down at his feet, grateful for what she's done but more grateful that Ruth cannot overhear these stark intimacies. He shuts the door and pushes down the catch.

Removing his shoes, he places them on the second stair alongside the toilet paper and toothpaste before creeping upstairs and along the landing to the bathroom. Without putting the light on, he pumps antiseptic handwash first on to one palm then the other, washes his hands with scalding water and dries them methodically, one finger at a time.

The bedroom, lit by a lamp standing on the chest of drawers, is airless and he opens the fanlight an inch or two behind the closed curtains. Ruth is watching him and he puts his finger to his lips as though they are conspirators. 'Margaret's gone. It's just us now.'

She smiles and tries to push herself up in the bed. 'Come and talk to me.' Her voice is stronger than it was this afternoon. 'What have you been doing?'

He dreads this question which she asks several times a day.

'Nothing' sounds as if he is wasting time – life's most precious commodity. 'I went for a walk' is as bad – a reminder of another thing she can no longer do.

He tries to be honest. 'I watched the news then Margaret made me go out and get some air. Said I look peaky.'

'News. I'd forgotten news. What's happening in the world?'

'The same old stuff.'

'No. Be specific. Tell me something real.' She sounds almost petulant.

He lies on the bed with his head on the pillow, touching hers. 'Let's think.' He pauses. A police siren sounds somewhere on the dual carriageway, a couple of streets away. 'Okay. There's this scruffy little dog … called Rags. He's black and white with a patch over one eye and –' he reaches across and strokes her cheek '– skinny legs. Like a barrel on matchsticks. Some sort of terrier. Anyway, yesterday, when his owner –'

'Male or female?'

'– when his owner, *Mrs Rich,* was taking him for a walk on the moor, out beyond the industrial estate, he took off after a rabbit. To cut a long story short, Rags fell down a disused mineshaft. Straight down. Couldn't get out.' He thinks back to the silent images of the couple on the beach and wonders where Mr. Rich was when his wife was dog-walking. 'Mrs. Rich ran miles to get help –'

'No mobile?'

'Battery dead. She flagged down a car and the driver gave her a lift to a phone box. She rang nine-nine-nine and the fire brigade turned out. They could hear Rags – poor little sod –

barking away, but the shaft was too narrow for a man to get down.' He closes his eyes and sees the distraught woman, chunky firemen in uniforms milling around behind her, at the mouth of the shaft; he hears the dog yapping from the darkness. 'The firemen decided that there wasn't much point in carrying on once it went dark so they packed up and went back to the fire station, intending to start again at first light tomorrow.' He visualises the windswept moor; dark; deserted; and hears the dog whimpering. 'Before they left, they threw some food down so Rags wouldn't be hungry.

'They'll get him out, won't they?' she whispers, turning her head and nuzzling his hand.

'Hang on, hang on. Just before I came up, there was a newsflash.' He pauses, feeling her slack body stiffen. 'Anyway, when Mrs Rich got home, guess what? Rags was on the doorstep.' He waits while first relief then puzzlement cross her face.

'But how?'

He imagines the dog, muddy and wet, bleeding from its front paw, but eyes shining and tail lashing at the sight of his beloved owner. Mrs Rich laughs and cries as Rags licks her face. 'They can't be sure but they think he must have found another shaft that brought him out further down the hillside. Apparently dogs' noses are very sensitive to air currents and he probably followed a draught.'

Ruth smiles and shuts her eyes. 'That's nice. A happy ending.'

'Yes.'

The bedside table is cluttered with the realities of her existence. Bottles of medicine and bubble-packed pills; a box of tissues; two feeding beakers with lids; wipes; mouthwash; a torch. And a small alarm clock, its slender red hand snatching away one second after the next.

# The Madonna
# at the Midland

**Patricia Duncker**

I should never have come. Some appalling sentimental delusion must have possessed me. Everything has changed. I've changed. Clarissa Dalloway sank into the mass of cushions and pillows strewn across her soundproofed bedroom at the Midland, overlooking the public library, closed for refurbishment, sprinkled eau de Cologne on her handkerchief and pressed it to her forehead. Where have I put the Nurofen? Did I bring it up from London? I should never have come. And indeed, even from this interesting position of supine luxury, the Manchester expedition did now smack of inevitable disaster.

Today is Saturday, and today is my 70th birthday. Sally will be 70 on Sunday. We always dreamed of being old ladies together, both war babies, born in '41, with identical memories, filling our hot water bottles from the tea urn in the school dining room, kicking our heels on those giant yellow radiators, trying on our new school uniforms in John Lewis, matching each other's footsteps in the frost. Our first birthday together and we celebrated with a bottle of Strongbow and a packet of Jaffa cakes and all the chocolate melted. I licked your fingers and you licked mine. I wore your jerseys and you wore my hats. I was two sizes smaller than you, so you couldn't get into my clothes. But you wrapped yourself up in my scarves and shawls. Your jerseys smelled of cinnamon, *Je reviens*, Hamlet cigars, you. You sat on the floor – yes, that is my first memory of Sally – you sat on the floor with your arms round your knees, smoking a cigarette. And you had that extraordinary beauty of the kind I most admired, dark, large-eyed, and that odd quality of abandonment, as if you could say anything, do anything and your beautiful voice made everything you said sound like a caress. We walked on the terrace before dinner, strolled past a stone urn overflowing with flowers. And you stopped, picked a flower, turned towards me, and kissed me on the lips. You kissed me.

Clarissa Dalloway seized her address book, the kiss still on her lips, peered at a row of faded numbers, chose the most recent, and snatched up the phone. *The number you have dialled has not been recognised, the number you have dialled has not been recognised, the number you have dialled...* She let the phone slide into the cushions. Twenty years. I haven't heard your voice in twenty years.

There had been cards at Christmas of course, and a skiing photograph from Vermont. There stood Sally, her face muffled in red scarves, poised and glamorous, amidst a mass of young men, her famous sons, all wielding their skis like machine guns, ready for the charge. I still have that photograph. But I have no children, and you are surrounded by sons. She rummaged in the sheets and bedspreads, as if Sally herself, or some of her fragrant belongings, lay burrowed against her cold thighs. What did I imagine? That a wealthy woman with five sons would welcome her elderly widowed friend, a friend she hasn't seen for twenty years, a trembling, tentative woman, frightened of her birthday and the long sigh of old age ahead. Her cleaning lady, Mrs B – for that was their little joke, Mrs B who does for Mrs D – at least she demonstrated some genuine interest. And how are you celebrating your birthday, Mrs D? And she had replied, all chipper and snappy, putting a brave face on things, I'm going up to Manchester to see an old friend. Well, isn't that nice, Mrs D. Good for you. Get you out a bit. And now here she was, cuddling a headache, disgruntled and ashamed, hiding her loneliness from her cleaning lady in a red terracotta palace of Grade II listed Edwardian magnificence, opened in 1903 and still going strong in a blaze of good-tempered elegance. *The number you have dialled has not been recognised.* She stumbled into the beige modernity of her tiled bathroom to avoid the rain, now leering into her bedroom, slicing down the windows, smirking at her through the white nets.

But here was Sally's voice again, booming through the little soaps and piles of towels. It always pours buckets in Manchester. Bring your brolly and galoshes, and if it eases up we'll pop out up the Peaks. Still got your walking shoes? We've got plenty of sticks and dogs! Do the whole thing in style with cream tea in Buxton at the end of the afternoon. Terrific. Why had she never travelled North? How can you lose touch with someone you love? Clarissa swallowed two Nurofen tablets, Extra Strength, and watched the water roaring into the bath. She had followed Richard abroad, given up her life for his career, as women once did, with everybody's blessing, trailed through compounds in Africa, smiled at a gift of snakes in Vietnam, played hostess at embassies in the Middle East where one day they were besieged with trays of sweetmeats, and the next evacuated in a fleet of armoured cars, racing through a torrent of explosions. Returning home to England, to the woodlands and orchards of Hampshire, flooded with calm and mossy lawns, she simply feared advancing beyond the French windows and the terrace, where she lurked, head down, guarded by goldenrod and Michaelmas daisies. Now I'm here, I won't move. And she was beginning to think just that once more, floating in the bath, disguised in foam. I've paid for the weekend. I'm here till Monday. I'll sit in the bath until Monday comes.

No, no, one more try. She scuttled back to the bed and stood dripping on a hand towel.

'Directory Enquiries please.'

'I'm sorry caller, the number you require is Ex-Directory.'

*The number you require…*

Clarissa Dalloway flung the phone back into the bedclothes, delighted. So she lives here still. And she still uses her own name. Get up, get dressed, get out. You might meet her in the street. Clarissa never considered how unlikely this was; she had picked up Sally's scent and was now fixed, like a bloodhound, head down, on the trail of her beloved. Forth she went in her green mackintosh and transparent rubber galoshes, twittering in the rain – what a lark! what a plunge! – determined to scout the art galleries, the bookshops, the pubs, like a knight seeking a damsel to rescue. In the end, defeated by drizzle, she mounted an extended attack on Harvey Nicholls, and spent three hours fingering lingerie, dress materials, ceramics, light autumn coats in the new colours, Scottish mist, Renaissance blue, that paradise blue of the Della Robbia Madonna, but buying nothing.

She confronted Saturday afternoon flat on her back, with the television whispering in the distance, wishing everything gone, vanished, annihilated, including every single one of her 70 years. This isn't what I longed for, hoped for, bought into. I've paid up my life's debts, and now I'm lonely and alone, washed up in a posh hotel bedroom with nothing, nothing, nothing. And is this all? Is this all there is? Towards six o'clock the rain increased, and fell in heavier, grey, vertical waves. She decided to change her ticket and return to London early the next day, and so she slid surreptitiously out of the Edwardian magnificence in her drenched green mackintosh, the galoshes grotesque upon her frumpish lace-up shoes.

*

Returning from Manchester Piccadilly, her first-class getaway return safely stashed in her purse, Clarissa Dalloway immediately noticed that something truly awful was taking place in the bowels of The Midland. A long queue of cars and taxis jostled before the great curves of the entrance on either side of the wyvern's extended claws. Lights, laughter, grey-slicked umbrellas shimmered through the drizzle. As she approached the ramp Clarissa saw two of the receptionists shaking with merriment and followed the line of their gaze.

King Kong and the Virgin Mary were climbing out of a taxi.

A very tall man in a gorilla suit ducked and bent before straightening to a colossal height. He nodded to the giggling receptionists; then let out a fearsome muffled roar and beat his chest. The Virgin Mary swatted his hairy arm. She stepped carefully onto the ramp, lifting her classic blue and white robes above the wet, and steadied her crown. This wobbling circular wire cage, which formed a most extraordinary fascinator, covered in glittering *papier mâché* fluorescent stars, floated in an arc above her head. Her veil fell back, graceful, folded away from her young, shining face. She mirrored every tacky nineteenth–century plastercast statue of the Blessed Virgin, worshipped right across Europe and sneered at by tourists. Clarissa shuddered. Had she walked straight into the yawning jaws of a fancy dress ball?

For indeed she had. Shrieks of disbelief and recognition erupted in the foyer. The Octagon terrace was roped off like a crime scene and the Trafford Room entirely commandeered for the event. A small passage still remained open for clients assaying the French restaurant. Clarissa scuttled in, shrunken inside her mackintosh and galoshes, a social sacrifice, unfashionable and demoralised. A hoard of revellers filled the foyer and laid siege to the Reception desks. She paused, walled in by smiles and jolly shouts. Clearly most of them were staying in the hotel. No rational pattern could be deduced from the costumes. She recognised Mae West in gold lamé and massive falsies, chatting to Marlene Dietrich, who posed, luscious in spangles, high heels, top hat and tails, showing a leg in black fishnet tights. The Blue Angel twirled before the crowd, so that her tails spun out behind her, scooped a cigarette lighter out of her tiny glittering evening bag, and actually lit up two cigarettes.

'Here you are, darling.' She handed one to Mae West. The Hotel Functions Director, pink with horrified amusement, ushered them out through the swing doors, deftly popping a purple feather boa round Mae West's massive bare shoulders.

'You can't smoke in here, ladies,' he grinned.

As they strode out Clarissa realised that both these glamorous stars of times past, were in fact, men. They paused to kiss Sherlock Holmes and Dr Watson, who arrived with an elegant young woman captured between them, as if under arrest. Her forties outfit, straight skirt, seamed stockings, wonderful cream shoes with block heels and a flower on each foot perched above her painted toes, gave no clue to the disguise. But she was hauling a large wooden Dalmatian on red wheels whose tail stood straight up like a mast.

'I'm supposed to have 100 more, you know,' she said, cheerfully addressing Clarissa, 'but what the hell. You're most mysterious. Can't guess at all. Who are you meant to be?'

But here were two young men in Tony Blair and Gordon

Brown masks, punching each other as they rolled into the foyer, and then a gang of friends, disgorged from three taxis, all dressed up as the entire cast of Coronation Street in its heyday, Elsie Tanner and an enormous Ena Sharples, tiny pink curlers clamped under his black hairnet, arm in arm, leading the ghastly crew. Clarissa, retreating in horror, bumped into Posh and Becks, or at least, a couple that looked exactly like the Beckhams, emerging from the lift. No, maybe the woman's hips curved in a more opulent undulation, Victoria Beckham's anorexic style blossoming into voluptuousness.

Clarissa Dalloway stood looking at this rippling mass of the young and the beautiful, however brazenly attired, and knew herself to be old.

The Director of Functions, Events, Banquets, Weddings and Ceremonies hovered at her elbow.

'Please forgive the disturbance, Mrs Dalloway. Lady Rosseter is holding a fancy dress ball for her family and friends.' Who on earth was Lady Rosseter?

Glorious above the crowd, standing on the rim of the Octagon, towered the couple who were clearly the hosts, older than their guests, yet more glamorous, the woman swish and gleaming in a 1930s ballgown, swathes of green silk, elbow-length white gloves, an authentic cap of red and green feathers, and several endless coils of pearls, ivory against the shimmering green. Who is this tall and vivid woman, heavily made up like an actress, a lorgnette vibrating on her bosom? The man beside her caught her arm.

'Darling, here they are! Both looking absolutely ridiculous.'

The suave impresario resembled someone famous. But who? A grey smoking jacket, all silk and velvet, the hair slicked back and the profile uncannily exact, ah! the pastiche voice has given his identity away. This is the Second Coming of Noel Coward. He might burst into *Mad Dogs and Englishmen* or *The Bar at the Piccola Marina* at any minute.

King Kong and the Virgin Mary bounced up the steps to hug them both. The hostess (for is this indeed Lady Rosseter?) pulled the ape's hairy ears and kissed the Virgin Mary with a jubilant smack, so that all her stars jiggled in the firmament. Clarissa heard every shouted word.

'Sweethearts, you've driven all this way. How divine! But you've missed the point entirely. And I did send you a list. You're supposed to come dressed up as famous people who stayed at the Midland, not as cinema monsters or Bible idols! Look at your brother and his boyfriend!' She pointed out two well-dressed Edwardian gentlemen, who were holding hands. 'That's the Honourable Charles Rolls and Mr Henry Royce, who met at the Midland, before going into business together. Just as they did!'

King Kong lifted his head off and the eyes went blank. A cheerful blonde face appeared.

'Doesn't matter, Mama. King Kong and the Blessed Virgin will be staying here tonight. You did book us a room, didn't you?'

The heady laugh and the extravagant gesture of affection were utterly familiar. The actress slipped her arm through that of the Madonna, and handed her a glass of champagne.

'My love, whatever possessed you to come as the Virgin Mary?

Benjamin has ape fantasies, and he's never been the same since he read Darwin at college, but you're not religious, are you?'

Unblushing, mischievous, the young woman in her blue and white robes more or less announced to all the Octagon, the foyer, even the passing guests in the Wyvern, bent on escaping the decorated mass of young people.

'An angel told me to do it! And to bring you the Good News. I'm pregnant!'

'Never!'

'Yup! Four months gone.'

The low rising whoop from the older woman, her shivering pearls, the wild triumphant grin, suddenly snapped into focus, a sharpened image, as if an old sepia photograph or a fuzzy shot of a skiing party resolved into digital Technicolor and High Definition. That laugh! That voice! Sally Seton! Sally Seton! After all these years, still flying high, showing off, glamorous, gorgeous, extraordinary! No one else ever laughed like that. This enormous exotic green serpent is my friend. This is the woman I came to Manchester to find. This is the woman I have not seen for two decades. This is the woman I loved.

Clarissa stood forgotten in the crowd, shocked, damp and horrified. I came here to find you Sally and I am dressed like an unemployed primary school teacher down on her luck. And if that is Noel Coward, then you are Gertrude Lawrence (*Private Lives, Hay Fever*, Oh God, all my parents' favourite plays), but we shall never manage to pull off even the briefest of encounters. Tonight is your night, not mine. I am Cinderella, unable to go to the ball.

Clarissa dashed for the lift.

Push the buttons. Quick. Carry me away in elderly shame to my luxury suite, where I shall call for Room Service, eat nothing but sandwiches, and escape in the morning before anyone else appears downstairs. Sally Seton. Sally Seton, the mother of sons. Bring forth men-children only. And that's just what Sally did. She had more testosterone in her little finger than most men have in their entire bodies. But I thought she'd married a miner's son, who'd earned every penny of his wealth, a balding manufacturer, not a Noel Coward look-alike.

Clarissa emerged on the fourth floor and wandered in aimless confusion, peering at the doors, before she realised her mistake.

Quick! Back to the lift. Second floor.

At first she didn't notice that someone else already stood inside the lift, leaning against the mirrors, reflected to eternity. But out of the edge of her eye she saw herself, in her evil green mackintosh and spattered handbag, accompanied by a figure in blue and white robes. The *papier mâché* stars seemed to have faded a little, the stick-on spangles reduced to a gentle, circular glow.

'Come back downstairs,' said the Virgin Mary. 'Sally's expecting you and hoping against hope that you'll come. She talked of nothing else last night. You are invited to the ball, and you ought to come.'

'I never received an invitation,' Clarissa addressed the image in the mirror.

'But you did. It came this morning. And Sally found your number too. She actually went through her contacts in the

Foreign Office. She rang. At once. Just at the moment you tried to ring her. And she spoke to Mrs B.'

'Mrs B?'

'Yes. And Mrs B told her that you were already on your way to Manchester, and that you were looking forward to celebrating your birthday with your oldest friend.'

The Virgin Mary chuckled.

'You should have heard her laugh. You always loved to hear her laugh.'

A brown hand slid forth from the Biblical sleeves, overrode the lift's commands and pressed Ground Floor. Clarissa gazed at the hand, transfixed, for it was not a young woman's hand; the skin, dehydrated and shrivelled, blotched with dark liver spots, the nails yellowed with age, flecks of soil engrained in the creases. This hand, a working woman's hand, a hand that had planted seeds, tended goats, hammered tent pegs into stony desert earth, now clamped firm upon the gleaming metal of futurity, this hand was as old as Solomon.

Clarissa recoiled from the hand in horror. The doors sprang open and she was ejected back into the foyer, straight into the arms of Winston Churchill, Luciano Pavarotti and Sarah Bernhardt, clearly impersonating Salomé, eyes black-rimmed with kohl, and carrying a snake. Pavarotti caught her handbag, steadied her gently and bowed.

'Scusi, Signorina.'

He bowed again. The vast stomach, held in place by a scarlet cummerbund, looked appallingly inauthentic. He peered at her closely.

'Aunt Clarissa? Yes, yes, it is you. Fabulous. Come quick. Mummy will be overjoyed!'

O Lord. The eldest son remembers me.

But as they approached the Octagon, Clarissa's whirling feet barely skimming the floor, Sally Seton, whose restless gaze interrogated every mad mask and hat, suddenly saw them coming and hurtled over the tapes, her face alight, her lips round and howling.

'Clarissa!'

A great screech of joy accompanied the embrace and Clarissa Dalloway swallowed a mouthful of green feathers.

'Shit,' cried Sally, 'my hat's come off!'

All on top of each other, embarrassed, laughing words tumbled out and Clarissa turned, with Sally's hand in hers, to see the rooms full of smiling hoards, to glimpse candlesticks on the bar, the trays of champagne buckets and glittering flutes, ready for the toast, the canapés nestling in lettuce and vine leaves, the blowing curtains, the night banished outside and Luciano Pavarotti, his black curls askew, presenting her with a gigantic bouquet of white roses.

'Happy Birthday, darling,' whispered Sally, twenty years of unspoken love blossoming in her extraordinary, abandoned smile.

For some reason the entire company began to clap. The guest of honour is come among us. Let the festivities begin.

Sally Seton gabbled in her ear.

'You must have a costume, my sweetheart, my angel. This'll go on all night and people will start asking who you are. At the

158

moment you look like that awful feminist who taught us at school, Miss Kilman in her mackintosh. Come upstairs. I've brought just the thing. I knew you wouldn't have time to sort it all out. Are you still two sizes smaller than I am? '

Unfortunately, not. Sally had expanded and Clarissa had shrunk. The sailor suit trousers were much too wide and had to be belted up, but the jaunty cap and blue Breton stripes fitted exactly.

'Well, at least our heads are still the same size.' Sally stood behind her, ogling their combined reflections. 'Do you remember? I always wore your hats and scarves.'

'Who am I supposed to be?'

'Daphne du Maurier of course. Gertrude's dearest friend. Friends for life they were. As we are.'

And she smothered Clarissa in pearls, silk, feathers and kisses.

'Come and meet Max. People keep calling him Lord Rosseter and he can't stand it.'

Sally Seton's husband stayed suave and in character as he looked her over, assessing her costume, like the director of the play.

'I say, you'll do splendidly old thing!' And he actually winked. 'Has everyone got a glass of champagne?'

He addressed the crowded Octagon.

'A formal speech of welcome to all our family and friends probably isn't appropriate tonight, and we all know why we're here, so I'll sing a song about a respectable British matron, who discovered in the nick of time that life was for living.'

Pavarotti, seated at the piano, let fly a little chaser up and down the scales; then without further ado Lord Rosseter burst into song – *The Bar at the Piccola Marina*. The bar, supposedly full of sailors enjoying a 'queer, unfamiliar atmosphere', addressed not only Clarissa's peculiar situation, but also her costume. She stealthily removed her elbow from the gleaming counter, adjusted her sailor's hat and tried not to look too obviously implicated. Sally's arm coiled about her waist. They arrived at the moment where everybody bellowed, *'Que bella Signorina!'* Pavarotti encouraged the party mass to join in and the song became a rousing chorus and duet. King Kong could be heard during a pause, shouting the line, 'Please come home Mama!' at Sally, who produced a wild shriek and clutched Clarissa, as if her beloved friend, so lately recaptured, was threatened with removal. 'Who do you think you are?' she yelled in riposte, with perfect timing. Everybody cheered. The *Piccola Marina* was evidently Lord Rosseter's party piece.

But he didn't stop there. No sooner had the cheers and shouts subsided than he exploded into an adapted version of *Let's Fall in Love*, and the eager amazement of the crowd told Clarissa that they were all hearing this version of the song for the first time.

*Sally Seton it is true took a more romantic view*
*Of this sly biological urge,*
*But it was really Max*
*In possession of the facts,*
*Who contrived to make their styles converge!*

Sally Seton let out a little sqeal of pleasure, leaned over and kissed Clarissa on the lips. The faint whiff of *Je reviens* assailed Clarissa's nostrils. She clutched the bar, as if electrocuted.

*He said: All Kings from Kong*
*Down to Ben do it*
*Others sing a song and then do it*
*Let's do it, let's fall in love!*

Clarissa sank down into her sailor suit, purple with embarrassment. Lord Rosseter had transformed himself into a cross between a satirical Calypso singer and a stand-up comedian. Everybody leaned forwards, desperate to hear the words and jeer at the people he teased.

*Dodie Smith and her dogs do it!*
(I say old chap, keep it clean, shouted Sherlock Holmes)
*Boys hidden in the bogs do it!*
(Oooooooh! A knowing queer chuckle radiated from the revellers)
*Let's do it, let's fall in love!*

*Detectives in hats do it!*
*Operatic acts do it!*
*Let's do it, let's fall in love!*
*Virgins with stars do it,*
*Rolls and Royce in cars do it!*

That's it! Something snapped into place in Clarissa's brain. Where is the Virgin Mary? She's responsible for all this. And how many of them are there? She could not absorb the significance of the uncanny encounter in the lift and searched the crowd, looking for two haloes. Across the strangely oriental space of the Octagon, Clarissa picked out a joyous *papier mâché* halo, the stars vibrating with satisfaction and righteousness. She peered at the face beneath the veil. Someone tapped her shoulder – the barman offering more champagne. As he filled her glass she noticed his hand. Wizened and misshapen, brown as an elderly monkey's claw, the ancient hand deftly withdrew the bottle. Clarissa spun round, her hat askew, to face a charming young man, his solicitous smile just slightly too well arranged. He wished her a Happy Birthday, his words suddenly lost in a roar of laughter. She was being watched. She had always been watched. There were many more than two of them.

# Leaves and Geese

## Sarah Jackman

I hear the front door closing. Gina must be going out for milk. Or maybe something we need for supper. If I sit forward I can watch her crossing the road. She has slipped her shoes on with bare feet and left her coat unbuttoned so that it flies behind her as she runs across. She has the carefree demeanour of a much younger woman.

Gina heads towards the community shop on the west side of the Common. You won't catch me using them if I can help it; everything's over-priced and I don't like being caught up with conversation when I just want to pay and get out. Gina says there's no obligation to chat and their friendliness is exactly why she prefers shopping there, plus she thinks it's important to support what they're doing.

While I wait for Gina to come back into view, I scan the Common with my binoculars in hope of spotting something of interest.

A jay bounces across the mown grass beneath the oak trees searching for acorns. The blue patch on its wing is radiant in the dull evening light which follows a flat autumn day. Leaves hang sullenly waiting for a good strong wind to set them loose.

When the trees are in full leaf, it's hard to believe that once they drop I'll have an unimpeded view to the ponds.

A pair of magpies frighten off the jay and strut around as if they own the place until my wife approaches. From the shape and weight of Gina's carrier bag I think it probably is milk she's bought and maybe a packet of homemade shortbread biscuits, if I'm lucky.

When Gina reaches the road I lower the binoculars and wave but she's preoccupied with watching for a gap in the traffic. I've lost count of the number of times I've asked her to use the crossing further down but she never does. A passing van blocks my view and an instant later reveals an empty pavement where Gina had stood. It's as if she's been erased.

I don't relax until Gina's safely back in the room.

'Got your favourites,' she announces. Gina's cheeks are pink from the cold air she's brought in and droplets of mist-moisture decorate strands of her hair. As she carries over the tray with mugs of tea and a plate of the shortbreads, I am assailed by a powerful scent of wood smoke, a smell which used to evoke happy memories and pleasant feelings but which I can't bear now.

About this time two years ago, some poor man set himself alight while sitting under the grand horse-chestnut which dominates our side of the Common.

At first I had thought kids were mucking around – burning a Guy Fawkes – until I saw the panic on people's faces. Somebody put the man out with a coat – badly burned his own hands doing it – but the man died anyway later in hospital. I couldn't get thoughts of him out of my head; the stench of burning permeated the house and hung around for days although Gina insisted it had gone. The local paper said it was suicide and you can only wonder at what would drive someone to such a desperate act. If you look, dark streaks still pattern the tree trunk where the bark was scorched.

'Number twelve's got a bonfire,' Gina says. 'There's smoke everywhere; you know how they always burn it too green.'

The smoke is drifting down the street, hazing the air. A shiver running through my body is stilled as Gina places her hands lightly on my shoulders and kisses the top of my head. The warmth awakened by her touch lingers long after the computer chirrups into life under her fingers.

Gina will spend hours on the computer – if I didn't interrupt her now and then, she probably wouldn't bother to take a break. She says she forgets the time. Since she's been working on the family tree she's made contact with relatives from all over the world and regularly exchanges news with a number of them.

As we lead a pretty quiet life, I wonder sometimes what she finds to talk about. 'Many small things make a bigger whole,' Gina says. This is more than a favourite phrase of my wife's; it's a personal philosophy which she happily applies to everything, including me, I don't doubt.

'Lucy's emailed. Kay, too.'

Kay is a distant Australian cousin for whom I can muster only mild interest but Lucy is our eldest grandchild and a delight to us both. Although she lives only half an hour's drive away, Lucy and Gina exchange almost daily emails. They've always been very close. Our youngest son, Steve, and his then girlfriend had Lucy when they were barely out of childhood themselves and they hit some pretty hefty bumps before splitting up for good. It was Gina who stepped up to take care of Lucy-loo until Steve was able to sort himself out.

'Lucy didn't get that job,' Gina says. 'But she's not upset. She says they weren't very friendly in the interview.'

'No loss there, then,' I reply but I find it barely conceivable that anyone could think to reject our lovely granddaughter.

I'm not keen on using computers, I prefer the feel of pen on paper, but when I have something to say to Lucy or one of the boys, I might add a line to the end of Gina's message. And Gina isn't averse to jotting the occasional entry in my journal either. Flicking back, I come across a couple of notes in her loose, chubby handwriting: *'2 men in long, black overcoats in August!!!'* *'1 male (wearing sunglasses), walking a Jack Russell with 3 legs.'* They make me smile now, which would have been Gina's intention at the time, I don't doubt, or perhaps in a gesture of conciliation following a tiff. Long forgotten.

Although little birdlife out of the ordinary shows its beak on the Common nowadays, today's page is full of appearances from various songbirds, starlings and corvids and the lively antics of the nuthatches and squirrels. I record the weather daily, too – at the end of the evening to give a full picture – and would agree wholeheartedly with the scientists that where the seasons and weather is concerned, something is afoot.

However, recently I've become more preoccupied with a

change in behaviour of the dominant life-form on the Common – the humans.

On a sunny weekend you could guarantee people would flock to the Common with chairs, blankets and a variety of balls, bats and whatnot, some with picnic paraphernalia, many feeding from the burger and ice cream vans that had tapped into this migratory habit. After a windy, autumn day, the tattered remains of kites would be flapping on telephone wires and in branches several weeks later. In winter a sprinkling of snow was bound to bring out the romance in couples who, wrapped up like Artic adventurers, made their way to the *Duke of Wellington* to steam up the windows and drip puddles of snow-melt onto the floor.

Now I've noticed a new breed in town. Like grey squirrels these are steadily nudging out the old species. With their financial muscle, big ideas and energy, they're shaping this landscape to their own liking. The food vans have been replaced by farmer's markets and the pub stands empty while people crowd the outside tables the length of High Street.

Gina is all for it. She likes the 'café culture'. She says that the children's garden and activity area would have been a blessing back in her day. She points out that I should be the first to support the efforts being made to improve the Common.

It's true that there's a lot to be pleased about: the bat and bird boxes they've put up will certainly help nesting rates and since the ponds were cleared and re-planted, the insect population has exploded; and the toad 'road patrols' really did reduce the carnage when the creatures were on the move.

Perhaps I am being sentimental over simpler times but the speed of change makes me nervous; I sense the cold detachment of a predator behind their smiles.

'Geese,' I say and Gina pauses her typing as the eerie whooping noise signals their approach. I wait for the birds to appear over the top of the house and hold my breath as they begin their descent to the ponds, only to arc away at the last moment.

I gaze at the journal which lies in readiness on my knee and it feels a little silly to record that nine Canada geese nearly landed. As I write I remember that the word for their flight is skein. A skein of geese. I write *skein* in my notebook. I write it again and again across the page. It's a lovely word. It makes me think of tumbling silk, of the lavender silk dressing gown Gina used to wear for summer breakfasts in the garden, and how it would slide open, revealing her thigh. Goose fits the landed bird, all that lumbering and honking. Not like my Gina of course. She's lost none of her elegance, still as graceful and light-footed as she's always been.

Gina says, 'Maybe in time, they'll start landing again.'

It's quiet now on the Common – family tea time before the joggers and dog walkers come out – and the brightest it's been all day. The sun has escaped the clouds and is sitting low behind the trees. I'm watching how the shifting light changes the colour of the grass from a vivid blue-green to a pale lichen tone when a strange thing happens.

Dozens of small brown birds fly up from the grass and form a spinning spiral of fluttering bodies a couple of feet above the ground and extending three, perhaps four feet into the air. Or maybe they are leaves caught up in a freak whirlwind. Even with binoculars it doesn't make sense. In all my life I've never seen birds behave this way and yet there's no sign of any wind in the trees.

A couple walking towards the bird-leaves appear oblivious to the scene ahead. It's as if they're visible only to me.

'Quick. Come here, Ginny.'

'Quick,' I repeat again as Gina takes her time, sighing and stretching as she rises from her chair.

'This had better not be one of your false alarms,' she warns as she takes the binoculars.

'Straight ahead. Do you see? What do you make of that?'

'What is it I'm supposed to be looking at?'

'Straight ahead. Over the grass.'

'I don't see anything,' Gina says slowly.

The shapes glitter like metal shavings as they criss-cross the spear of sunlight which has forged through a gap in the trees.

I'm beginning to panic that it's all in my head when Gina says, 'Oh my, how strange.'

'What do you think they are, darling? Birds or leaves?'

'Oh, birds definitely,' Gina says, then seconds later. 'No. Leaves, more than likely.' She hands me back the binoculars. 'I really can't tell Jack, you'd better take another look.'

But the bird-leaves have vanished. Clouds have drawn across the sun and the night has surged forward.

'It's over.'

'There wasn't a breath of wind when I went out to the shop.'

Gina's voice is thoughtful but in the next moment she has spun away and is back at her desk. One foot swings gently; I glimpse the shine of pearly painted toenails.

'I've never seen birds act like that, though. Have you, Ginny?'

'No, never. But perhaps they do. Perhaps it's secret bird stuff that we don't usually get to see, that they do when we're not looking.'

I don't reply. I lean back in the chair and dunk my biscuit in my tea. A drop lands on my open journal. I dab at the stain blurring the word 'skein' with the cuff of my sweater.

'But aren't you curious?' I'm not ready to leave the matter alone and rather irritated by the ease with which Gina seems to have shaken herself free.

'Not really. Actually, not at all.' Gina looks across at me. 'These days I find there's less and less that I'm willing to give more than a cursory glance to. Time is too precious. You have to let the rest go.'

Gina's words drift like restless, sorrowful birds around the room.

Is that how she does it? Is that her secret to seeming so serene, so certain? Each day the world seems to me a little more complicated, a notion more unfathomable. My attempts to grip on can leave me covered in a cold sweat of shame. Sometimes the fear of how we'll manage when ill-health and frailty strike keeps me from looking Gina in the eye.

I cast a glance her way. I might not be able to take care of you, I think, and the words sit like salt on the tip of my tongue. I might let you down.

'But you know what, love?' Gina's voice is soft, as if it's travelled a long way to reach me. 'It was an odd and beautiful thing, whatever it was. And I'm glad we saw it.'

'Yes,' I say and my eyes are drawn once more to the Common outside. A lone goose flies out of the shadows and begins a slow, silent circle above the ponds. In the moment before it dips to land I see its black silhouette sketched on the grey sky.

# Author biographies

**Zillah Bethell** lives in South Wales. Her first two novels *Seahorses are Real* and *Le Temps des Cerises* are published by Seren. She is currently working on her third book *Woman in a Dandelion Paperweight*.

**Dilys Cadwaladr** (19 March 1902 – January 1979) was a Welsh writer and poet. She is notable for being the first woman ever to win the crown at the National Eisteddfod of Wales. She achieved this feat in 1953 at Rhyl.

**Siân Melangell Dafydd** is an author, poet, translator and co-editor of *Taliesin*. Originally from Llwyneinion, Merionethshire, she studied History of Art at St Andrews University and worked in galleries in London and Europe before completing an MA in Creative Writing at the University of East Anglia. Her novel, *Y Trydydd Peth (The Third Thing)*, won the 2009 National Eisteddfod Literature Medal. She has published in many anthologies in Wales and abroad. In 2010 she won a Translators' House Wales-HALMA award and held residences in Finland and Germany. A collaborative work with poet Damian Walford Davies and photographer Paul White was published in spring 2012, *Ancestral Houses: The Lost Mansions of Wales/Tai Mawr a Mieri: Plastai Coll Cymru.*

**Patricia Duncker** is the author of five novels and two collections of short fiction including *Hallucinating Foucault* (1996), winner of the McKitterick Prize and the Dillons First Fiction Award, and *Miss Webster and Chérif* (2006) shortlisted for the Commonwealth Writers Prize, 2007. Her fifth novel, *The Strange Case of the Composer and his Judge* (Bloomsbury, 2010), was shortlisted for the CWA Golden Dagger award for the Best Crime Novel of the Year. Her critical work includes a collection of essays on writing, theory and contemporary literature, *Writing on the Wall* (2002). She is Professor of Contemporary Literature at the University of Manchester. She has lived in Aberystwyth for over twenty years. www.patriciaduncker.com

**Sarah Jackman** was born in Berlin and has lived variously in England, Germany and France. She moved to south Wales in 2004 and now lives near Neath. Sarah has published four novels: *Summer Circles* (2010), *Never Stop Looking* (2009), *The Other Lover* (2007) and *Laughing as they Chased Us* (2005) all by Simon & Schuster UK. Her short stories have appeared in a number of anthologies including Honno and World Wide Writers. Sarah is currently working on her next novel and a nature writing project. More details about Sarah and her writing can be found on: http://sarahjackman.com and her nature writing blog: http://writeaboutnature.com.

**Siân James** has written thirteen novels and two books of short stories. Her first two novels each won a Yorkshire Post prize and her first book of short stories *Not Singing Exactly*, published by Honno, won the Welsh Arts Council Book of the Year in 1997.

**Jane Anne Jones**: her use of daring and highly personal themes drove Louie Myfanwy Davies (1908–68) to use the pseudonym Jane Ann Jones. *Pererinion* is a bittersweet autobiographical novella about the relationship of a young girl with a married man. The original typescript was burned by the author's former lover, but the copy published here (for the first time ever in English) was discovered by Nan Griffiths in 2003. *Storïau Hen Ferch* (1937) features adulterous, unmarried, creative and brave women, and the author excels at examining the internal dynamics of everyday relationships.

**Angharad Penrhyn Jones** lives in Machynlleth, mid Wales, where she works as a freelance writer, editor and critic. She is also a campaigner and commentator on environmental issues. Born in London to a Welsh father and Swedish mother, she was educated in Flintshire through the medium of Welsh. She won a scholarship to study English Literature at Aberystwyth University, and after graduating she was shortlisted for the Observer Young Travel Writer of the Year award. She then joined an independent television company, where she produced and directed award-winning documentaries in collaboration with her twin sister, Sara. Over the years she has written for a wide range of publications, including the *Guardian*, *Mslexia*, *Planet* and *New Welsh Review*. In 2011 she won the Welsh-language Awel Aman Tawe poetry prize, and in the same year she received a Literature Wales bursary to complete her debut novel, which was recently taken up by a literary agent. This year she has written a puppet show for children, and she is also co-editing a Honno anthology about political campaigners. When she isn't working or caring for her daughter, she likes to walk along the Dyfi river and play the piano.

**Jo Mazelis** is a writer of short stories, non fiction and poetry. Her collection of stories *Diving Girls* (Parthian, 2002) was shortlisted for The Commonwealth Best First Book and Welsh Book of the Year. Her second book, *Circle Games* (Parthian, 2005) was longlisted for Welsh Book of the Year. She was born in Swansea where she currently lives. Originally trained at Art School, she worked for many years in London in magazine publishing as a freelance photographer, designer and illustrator, where she also began her writing career, producing short pieces on Lee Miller, Sylvia Plath, Gwen John and Paula Rego amongst others. She hopes her first novel and a new collection of stories will be published in 2013.

**Catherine Merriman** is the author of five novels and three collections of short stories. Her first novel (*Leaving the Light On*) won the Ruth Hadden Memorial prize for best first work (1991) and many of her stories have been broadcast on Radio 4. She is also the editor of the anthology *Laughing Not*

*Laughing* (2004), in which Welsh women write about their experience of sex. She lectures in creative writing at the University of Glamorgan. She lives near Abergavenny in Monmouthshire and is a Fellow of the Welsh Academy.

**Francesca Rhydderch**'s short stories have been published in *New Welsh Review* and *Planet: The Welsh Internationalist*, and broadcast on Radio 4 and Radio Wales. Her first novel, *The Rice Paper Diaries*, will be published by Seren in 2013. She lives in Aberystwyth.

**Catriona Stewart** has lived and worked in mid Wales for a quarter of a century. After a career in housing and customer services, where she occasionally made time for writing during career breaks with four children, she took early retirement and can now write as much as she wants. She's been successful in various short story competitions, including a first prize in the Costa/*Woman & Home* annual short story competition in 2009. She's working on a novel, or two, as well.

**Sarah Todd Taylor** moved from Yorkshire to Ceredigion at the age of eight. Her short stories have featured in several of Honno's previous anthologies and she has had a short monologue produced by BBC Radio Five Live. She works in education and spends her spare time singing opera.

**Jo Verity** started writing in 1999 'to see if she could'. Since then she has published four novels – *Not Funny, Not Clever*,

*Sweets from Morocco*, *Bells* and *Everything in the Garden* – all with Honno Welsh Women's Press. She won the *Richard & Judy Short Story Prize* (2003) and the *Western Mail* Short Story Competition (2004). She was a runner up in the *Mslexia* International Short Story Competition (2009) and the Rhys Davies Short Story Competition (2011). Jo lives in Cardiff and is currently working on her fifth novel.

## More from Honno

*Short stories; Classics; Autobiography; Fiction*

Founded in 1986 to publish the best of women's writing,
Honno publishes a wide range of titles from Welsh women.

## Honno anthologies

**All Shall be Well**, edited by *Penny Thomas* and *Stephanie Tillotson*
Honno's 25th anniversary anthology, brings together a wonderful and
absorbing collection of writing by Welsh women taken from the
fiction and non-fiction anthologies published by the press over the last
quarter of a century.

### *Non-fiction*

**In Her Element**, edited by *Jane MacNamee*
20 women writers from all over Wales recount their deep personal
connections to the landscapes which have shaped their lives – their
loves, their joys, their losses, their inner and their outer worlds...

**Strange Days Indeed**, edited by *Patricia Duncker* and *Janet Thomas*
Funny, shocking and tender, this is a unique collection of autobiographical
writings about motherhood penned by women from Wales.

**Laughing not Laughing**, edited by *Catherine Merriman*
A unique autobiographical collection of from 26 authors writing
about their sexual experiences. These accounts are compelling and
honest, and will variously entertain, inform, move, and on occasion,
shock the reader.

*Short fiction*

**Wooing Mr Wickham**

The winning stories from the 2010 Short Story Competition inspired by Jane Austen and Chawton House. Judged and introduced by award winning novelist Michèle Roberts.

**Cut on the Bias**, edited by *Stephanie Tillotson*

An anthology of fictional short stories that explores the intensely personal relationships women have with what they wear.

**Dancing with Mr Darcy**

Stories inspired by Jane Austen and Chawton House. An anthology of the winning entries in the Jane Austen Short Story Award 2009, selected by Sarah Waters, which celebrates the bicentenary of Jane Austen's arrival in the village of Chawton, where she spent most of her literary life.

**Getting a Life,** *Catherine Merriman*

Mammary orgasmic potential, atoms and molecules, the pursuit of beauty, the truth about art? These short stories are inhabited by characters all grappling with the "getting" of a life. A combination of the poignant, pitiless, hilarious and distinctly risky.

**Welsh Women's Classics**

*A unique series which brings great books by women writers from Wales, long since out of print, to a new generation of readers. There are now 20 Classics available in both English and Welsh.*

**Stranger Within The Gates**: A collection of short stories by *Bertha Thomas*, ed.*Kirsti Bohata*

First published in 1912, this is a collection of witty, sharply observed short stories. Bertha Thomas lightly but deftly sketches her characters with a sharp eye for humorous and satirical detail. Her stories are by turns Gothic, romantic, humorous, fantastic, satirical but always engagingly written.

## Clasuron Honno
### Pererinion a Storïau Hen Ferch
by **Jane Ann Jones**, gol. *Cathryn A. Charnell-White*
Ysgrifennai Louie Myfanwy Davies (1908–68) o dan y ffugenw Jane
Ann Jones am ei bod yn trafod themâu mor feiddgar a phersonol.
Nofela hunangofiannol chwerwfelys ynghylch perthynas merch ifanc â
dyn priod yw Pererinion. Mae'r awdur ar ei gorau yn archwilio
ymwneud pobl â'i gilydd.

## Honno fiction
### Eden's Garden, *Juliet Greenwood*
Sometimes you have to run away, sometimes you have to come home.
Two women a century apart struggle with love, family duty, long
buried secrets, and their own creative ambitions.

### Not Funny Not Clever, *Jo Verity*
Two middle-aged women, one handsome tv star and three teenagers:
Elizabeth was hoping for a week of wine and chat, Diane for help with
her dilemma and Jordan certainly wasn't planning to spend a week
with a substitute grandmother. With a bittersweet touch Jo Verity
throws a smorgasbord of characters together to work out what makes
life worth living.

All Honno titles can be ordered online at
**www.honno.co.uk**
twitter.com/honno
facebook.com/honnopress

## ABOUT HONNO

Honno Welsh Women's Press was set up in 1986 by a group of women who felt strongly that women in Wales needed wider opportunities to see their writing in print and to become involved in the publishing process. Our aim is to develop the writing talents of women in Wales, give them new and exciting opportunities to see their work published and often to give them their first 'break' as a writer. Honno is registered as a community co-operative. Any profit that Honno makes is invested in the publishing programme. Women from Wales and around the world have expressed their support for Honno. Each supporter has a vote at the Annual General Meeting. For more information and to buy our publications, please write to Honno at the address below, or visit our website: www.honno.co.uk

Honno, 14 Creative Units, Aberystwyth Arts Centre,
Aberystwyth, Ceredigion SY23 3GL

Honno Friends
We are very grateful for the support of the Honno Friends:
Gwyneth Tyson Roberts, Jenny Sabine, Beryl Thomas.

For more information on how you can become a Honno
Friend, see: http://www.honno.co.uk/friends.php